EX LIBRIS

CALUM Montgomery
NAME

BOOK THE SECOND

# THE REPTILE ROOM

# A Series of Unfortunate Events

BOOK THE SECOND

# THE REPTILE ROOM

by

*Lemony Snicket*

Illustrated by
BRETT HELQUIST

TED SMART

First published in the USA 1999
by HarperCollins Children's Books
This edition published in Great Britain 2001
by Egmont Books Ltd
239 Kensington High Street, London W8 6SA
for The Book People Ltd
Hall Wood Avenue, Haydock, St Helens WA11 9UL

Published by arrangement with HarperCollins
Children's Books,
a division of HarperCollins Publishers, Inc., New
York, New York, USA

Text copyright © 1999 Lemony Snicket
Inside illustration copyright © 1999 Brett Helquist
Cover illustration copyright © 2001 Brett Helquist

The moral right of the cover illustrator has been
asserted

ISBN 0 7497 4882 6

10 9 8 7 6 5 4 3 2 1

A CIP catalogue record for this title is available from
the British Library

Printed and bound in Italy

For Beatrice –
My love for you shall live forever.
You, however, did not.

# One

The stretch of road that leads out of the city, past Hazy Harbor and into the town of Tedia, is perhaps the most unpleasant in the world. It is called Lousy Lane. Lousy Lane runs through fields that are a sickly gray color, in which a handful of scraggly trees produce apples so sour that one only has to look at them to feel ill. Lousy Lane traverses the Grim River, a body of water that is nine-tenths mud and that contains extremely unnerving fish, and it encircles a horseradish factory, so the entire area smells bitter and strong.

I am sorry to tell you that this story begins with the Baudelaire orphans traveling along this most displeasing road, and that from this moment on, the story only gets worse. Of all the people in the world who have miserable lives—and, as I'm sure you know, there are quite a few—the Baudelaire youngsters take the cake, a phrase which here means that more horrible things have happened to them than just about anybody. Their misfortune began with an enormous fire that destroyed their home and killed both their loving parents, which is enough sadness to last anyone a lifetime, but in the case of these three children it was only the bad beginning. After the fire, the siblings were sent to live with a distant relative named Count Olaf, a terrible and greedy man. The Baudelaire parents had left behind an enormous fortune, which would go to the children when Violet came of age, and Count Olaf was so obsessed with getting his filthy hands on the money that he hatched a devious plan that gives me nightmares to this day. He was caught just in time, but he escaped and vowed to get ahold of the Baudelaire fortune sometime in the future. Violet, Klaus, and Sunny still had nightmares about Count Olaf's shiny, shiny eyes, and about his one scraggly eyebrow, and most of all about the tattoo of an eye he had on his ankle. It seemed like that eye was watching the Baudelaire orphans wherever they went.

So I must tell you that if you have opened this book in the hope of finding out that the children lived happily ever after, you might as well shut it and read something else. Because Violet, Klaus, and Sunny, sitting in a small, cramped car and staring out the windows at Lousy Lane, were heading toward even more misery and woe. The Grim River and the horseradish factory were only the first of a sequence of tragic and unpleasant episodes that bring a frown to my face and a tear to my eye whenever I think about them.

The driver of the car was Mr. Poe, a family friend who worked at a bank and always had a cough. He was in charge of overseeing the orphans' affairs, so it was he who decided that the children would be placed in the care of a distant relative in the country after all the unpleasantness with Count Olaf.

"I'm sorry if you're uncomfortable," Mr. Poe said, coughing into a white handkerchief, "but this new car of mine doesn't fit too many people. We couldn't even fit any of your suitcases. In a week or so I'll drive back here and bring them to you."

"Thank you," said Violet, who at fourteen was the oldest of the Baudelaire children. Anyone who knew Violet well could see that her mind was not really on what Mr. Poe was saying, because her long hair was tied up in a ribbon to keep it out of her eyes. Violet was an inventor, and when she was thinking up inventions she liked to tie her hair up this way. It helped her think clearly about the various gears, wires, and ropes involved in most of her creations.

"After living so long in the city," Mr. Poe continued, "I think you will find the countryside to be a pleasant change. Oh, here is the turn. We're almost there."

"Good," Klaus said quietly. Klaus, like many people on car rides, was very bored, and he was sad not to have a book with him. Klaus loved to read, and at approximately twelve years of age had read more books than many people read in their whole lives. Sometimes he read well into the night, and in the morning could be found fast asleep, with a book in his hand and his glasses still on.

"I think you'll like Dr. Montgomery, too," Mr. Poe said. "He has traveled a great deal, so he has plenty of stories to tell. I've heard his house is filled with things he's brought from all the places he's been."

"Bax!" Sunny shrieked. Sunny, the youngest of the Baudelaire orphans, often talked like this, as infants tend to do. In fact, besides biting things with her four very sharp teeth, speaking in fragments was how Sunny spent most of her time. It was often difficult to tell what she meant to say. At this moment she probably meant something along the lines of "I'm nervous about meeting a new relative." All three children were.

"How exactly is Dr. Montgomery related to us?" Klaus asked.

"Dr. Montgomery is—let me see—your late father's cousin's wife's brother. I think that's right. He's a scientist of some sort, and receives a great deal of money from the government." As a banker, Mr. Poe was always interested in money.

"What should we call him?" Klaus asked.

"You should call him Dr. Montgomery," Mr. Poe replied, "unless he tells you to call him Montgomery. Both his first and last names are Montgomery, so it doesn't really make much difference."

"His name is Montgomery Montgomery?" Klaus said, smiling.

"Yes, and I'm sure he's very sensitive about that, so don't ridicule him," Mr. Poe said, coughing again into his handkerchief. "'Ridicule' means 'tease.'"

Klaus sighed. "I *know* what 'ridicule' means," he said. He did not add that of course he also knew not to make fun of someone's name. Occasionally, people thought that because the orphans were unforunate, they were also dim-witted.

Violet sighed too, and took the ribbon out of her hair. She had been trying to think up an invention that would block the smell of horseradish from reaching one's nose, but she was too nervous about meeting Dr. Montgomery to focus on it. "Do you know what sort of scientist he is?" she asked. She was thinking Dr. Montgomery might have a laboratory that would be of use to her.

"I'm afraid not," Mr. Poe admitted. "I've been very busy making the arrangements for you three, and I didn't have much time for chit-chat. Oh, here's the driveway. We've arrived."

Mr. Poe pulled the car up a steep gravel driveway and toward an enormous stone house. The house had a square front door made of dark wood, with several columns marking the front porch. To each side of the door were lights in the shapes of torches, which were brightly lit even though it was morning. Above the front door, the house had rows and rows of square windows, most of which were open to let in the breeze. But in front of the house was what was truly unusual: a vast, well-kept lawn, dotted with long, thin shrubs in remarkable shapes. As Mr. Poe's car came to a halt, the Baudelaires could see that the shrubs had been trimmed so as to look like snakes. Each hedge was a different kind of serpent, some long, some short, some with their tongues out and some with their mouths open, showing green, fearsome teeth. They were quite eerie, and Violet, Klaus, and Sunny were a bit hesitant about walking beside them on their way up to the house.

Mr. Poe, who led the way, didn't seem to notice the hedges at all, possibly because he was busy coaching the children on how to behave.

"Now, Klaus, don't ask too many questions right away. Violet, what happened to the ribbon in your hair? I thought you looked very distinguished in it. And somebody please make sure Sunny doesn't bite Dr. Montgomery. That wouldn't be a good first impression."

Mr. Poe stepped up to the door and rang a doorbell that was one of the loudest the children had ever heard. After a moment's pause, they could hear approaching footsteps, and Violet, Klaus, and Sunny all looked at one another. They had no way of knowing, of course, that very soon there would be more misfortune within their unlucky family, but they nevertheless felt uneasy. *Would Dr. Montgomery be a kind person?* they wondered. *Would he at least be better than Count Olaf? Could he possibly be worse?*

The door creaked open slowly, and the Baudelaire orphans held their breath as they peered into the dark entryway. They saw a dark burgundy carpet that lay on the floor. They saw a stained-glass light fixture that dangled from the ceiling. They saw a large oil painting of two snakes entwined together that hung on the wall. But where was Dr. Montgomery?

"Hello?" Mr. Poe called out. "Hello?"

"Hello hello hello!" a loud voice boomed out, and from behind the door stepped a short, chubby man with a round red face. "I am your Uncle Monty, and this is really perfect timing! I just finished making a coconut cream cake!"

"*Doesn't* Sunny like coconut?" Uncle Monty asked. He, Mr. Poe, and the Baudelaire orphans were all sitting around a bright green table, each with a slice of Uncle Monty's cake. Both the kitchen and the cake were still warm from baking. The cake was a magnificent thing, rich and creamy with the perfect amount of coconut. Violet, Klaus, and Uncle Monty were almost finished with their pieces, but Mr. Poe and Sunny had taken only one small bite each.

"To tell you the truth," Violet said, "Sunny doesn't really like anything soft to eat. She prefers very hard food."

"How unusual for a baby," Uncle Monty said, "but not at all unusual for many snakes. The Barbary Chewer, for example, is a snake that must have something in its mouth at all times, otherwise it begins to eat its own mouth. Very difficult to keep in captivity. Would Sunny perhaps like a raw carrot? That's plenty hard."

"A raw carrot would be perfect, Dr. Montgomery," Klaus replied.

The children's new legal guardian got up and walked toward the refrigerator, but then turned around and wagged a finger at Klaus. "None of that 'Dr. Montgomery' stuff," he said. "That's way too stuffy for me. Call me Uncle Monty! Why, my fellow herpetologists don't even call me Dr. Montgomery."

"What are herpetologists?" Violet asked.

"What do they call you?" Klaus asked.

"Children, children," Mr. Poe said sternly. "Not so many questions."

Uncle Monty smiled at the orphans. "That's quite all right," he said. "Questions show an inquisitive mind. The word 'inquisitive' means—"

"We know what it means," Klaus said. "'Full of questions.'"

"Well, if you know what that means," Uncle Monty said, handing a large carrot to Sunny, "then you should know what herpetology is."

"It's the study of something," Klaus said. "Whenever a word has *ology*, it's the study of something."

"Snakes!" Uncle Monty cried. "Snakes, snakes, snakes! That's what I study! I love snakes, all kinds, and I circle the globe looking for different kinds to study here in my laboratory! Isn't that interesting?"

"That *is* interesting," Violet said, "*very* interesting. But isn't it dangerous?"

"Not if you know the facts," Uncle Monty said. "Mr. Poe, would you like a raw carrot as well? You've scarcely touched your cake."

Mr. Poe turned red, and coughed into his handkerchief for quite some time before replying, "No, thank you, Dr. Montgomery."

Uncle Monty winked at the children. "If you like, you may call me Uncle Monty as well, Mr. Poe."

"Thank you, Uncle Monty," Mr. Poe said stiffly. "Now, *I* have a question, if you don't mind. You mentioned that you circle the globe. Is there someone who will come and take care of the children while you are out collecting specimens?"

"We're old enough to stay by ourselves," Violet said quickly, but inside she was not so sure. Uncle Monty's line of work did sound interesting, but she wasn't sure if she was ready to stay alone with her siblings, in a house full of snakes.

"I wouldn't hear of it," Uncle Monty said. "You three must come with me. In ten days we leave for Peru, and I want you children right there in the jungle with me."

"Really?" Klaus said. Behind his glasses, his eyes were shining with excitement. "You'd really take us to Peru with you?"

"I will be glad to have your help," Uncle Monty said, reaching over to take a bite of Sunny's piece of cake. "Gustav, my top assistant, left an unexpected letter of resignation for me just yesterday. There's a man named Stephano whom I have hired to take his place, but he won't arrive for a week or so, so I am way behind on preparations for the expedition. Somebody has to make sure all the snake traps are working, so I don't hurt any of our specimens. Somebody has to read up on the terrain of Peru so we can navigate through the jungle without any trouble. And somebody has to slice an enormous length of rope into small, workable pieces."

"I'm interested in mechanics," Violet said, licking her fork, "so I would be happy to learn about snake traps."

"I find guidebooks fascinating," Klaus said, wiping his mouth with a napkin, "so I would love to read up on Peruvian terrain."

"Eojip!" Sunny shrieked, taking a bite of carrot. She probably meant something along the lines of "I would be thrilled to bite an enormous length of rope into small, workable pieces!"

"Wonderful!" Uncle Monty cried. "I'm glad you have such enthusiasm. It will make it easier to do without Gustav. It was very strange, his leaving like that. I was unlucky to lose him." Uncle Monty's face clouded over, a phrase which here means "took on a slightly gloomy look as Uncle Monty thought about his bad luck," although if Uncle Monty had known what bad luck was soon to come, he wouldn't have wasted a moment thinking about Gustav. I wish—and I'm sure you wish as well—that we could go back in time and warn him, but we can't, and that is that. Uncle Monty seemed to think that was that as well, as he shook his head and smiled, clearing his brain of troubling thoughts.

"Well, we'd better get started. No time like the present, I always say. Why don't you show Mr. Poe to his car, and then I'll show you to the Reptile Room."

The three Baudelaire children, who had been so anxious when they had walked through the snake-shaped hedges the first time, raced confidently through them now as they escorted Mr. Poe to his automobile.

"Now, children," Mr. Poe said, coughing into his handkerchief, "I will be back here in about a week with your luggage and to make sure everything is all right. I know that Dr. Montgomery might seem a bit intimidating to you, but I'm sure in time you will get used to—"

"He doesn't seem intimidating at all," Klaus interrupted. "He seems very easy to get along with."

"I can't wait to see the Reptile Room," Violet said excitedly.

"Meeka!" Sunny said, which probably meant "Good-bye, Mr. Poe. Thank you for driving us."

"Well, good-bye," Mr. Poe said. "Remember, it is just a short drive here from the city, so please contact me or anyone else at Mulctuary Money Management if you have any trouble. See you soon." He gave the orphans an awkward little wave with his handkerchief, got into his small car, and drove back down the steep gravel driveway onto Lousy Lane. Violet, Klaus, and Sunny waved back, hoping that Mr. Poe would remember to roll up the car windows so the stench of horseradish would not be too unbearable.

*"Bambini!"* Uncle Monty cried out from the front door. "Come along, bambini!"

The Baudelaire orphans raced back through the hedges to where their new guardian was waiting for them. *"Violet,* Uncle Monty," Violet said. "My name is Violet, my brother's is Klaus, and Sunny is our baby sister. None of us is named Bambini."

"'Bambini' is the Italian word for 'children,'" Uncle Monty explained. "I had a sudden urge to speak a little Italian. I'm so excited to have you three here with me, you're lucky I'm not speaking gibberish."

"Have you never had any children of your own?" Violet asked.

"I'm afraid not," Uncle Monty said. "I always meant to find a wife and start a family, but it just kept slipping my mind. Shall I show you the Reptile Room?"

"Yes, please," Klaus said.

Uncle Monty led them past the painting of snakes in the entryway into a large room with a grand staircase and very, very high ceilings. "Your rooms will be up there," Uncle Monty said, gesturing up the stairs. "You can each choose whatever room you like and move the furniture around to suit your taste. I understand that Mr. Poe has to bring your luggage later in that puny car of his, so please make a list of anything you might need and we'll go into town tomorrow and buy it so you don't have to spend the next few days in the same underwear."

"Do we really each get our own room?" Violet asked.

"Of course," Uncle Monty said. "You don't think I'd coop you all up in one room when I have this enormous house, do you? What sort of person would do that?"

"Count Olaf did," Klaus said.

"Oh, that's right, Mr. Poe told me," Uncle Monty said, grimacing as if he had just tasted something terrible. "Count Olaf sounds like an awful person. I hope he is torn apart by wild animals someday. Wouldn't that be satisfying? Oh, well, here we are: the Reptile Room."

Uncle Monty had reached a very tall wooden door with a large doorknob right in the middle of it. It was so high up that he had to stand on his tiptoes to open it. When it swung open on its creaky hinges, the Baudelaire orphans all gasped in astonishment and delight at the room they saw.

The Reptile Room was made entirely out of glass, with bright, clear glass walls and a high glass ceiling that rose up to a point like the inside of a cathedral. Outside the walls was a bright green field of grasses and shrubs which was of course perfectly visible through the transparent walls, so standing in the Reptile Room was like being inside and outside at the same time. But as remarkable as the room itself was, what was inside the Reptile Room was much more exciting. Reptiles, of course, were lined up in locked metal cages that sat on wooden tables in four neat rows all the way down the room. There were all sorts of snakes, naturally, but there were also lizards, toads, and assorted other animals that the children had never seen before, not even in pictures, or at the zoo. There was a very fat toad with two wings coming out of its back, and a two-headed lizard that had bright yellow stripes on its belly. There was a snake that had three mouths, one on top of the other, and another that seemed to have no mouth at all. There was a lizard that looked like an owl, with wide eyes that gazed at them from the log on which it was perched in its cage, and a toad that looked just like a church, complete with stained-glass eyes. And there was a cage with a white cloth on top of it, so you couldn't see what was inside at all. The children walked down the aisles of cages, peering into each one in amazed silence. Some of the creatures looked friendly, and some of them looked scary, but all of them looked fascinating, and the Baudelaires took a long, careful look at each one, with Klaus holding Sunny up so she could see.

The orphans were so interested in the cages that they didn't even notice what was at the far end of the Reptile Room until they had walked the length of each aisle, but once they reached the far end they gasped in astonishment and delight once more. For here, at the end of the rows and rows of cages, were rows and rows of bookshelves, each one stuffed with books of different sizes and shapes, with a cluster of tables, chairs, and reading lamps in one corner. I'm sure you remember that the Baudelaire children's parents had an enormous collection of books, which the orphans remembered fondly and missed dreadfully, and since the terrible fire, the children were always delighted to meet someone who loved books as much as they did. Violet, Klaus, and Sunny examined the books as carefully as they had the reptile cages, and realized immediately that most of the books were about snakes and other reptiles. It seemed as if every book written on reptiles, from *An Introduction to Large Lizards* to *The Care and Feeding of the Androgynous Cobra*, were lined up on the shelves, and all three children, Klaus especially, looked forward to reading up on the creatures in the Reptile Room.

"This is an amazing place," Violet said finally, breaking the long silence.

"Thank you," Uncle Monty said. "It's taken me a lifetime to put together."

"And are we really allowed to come inside here?" Klaus asked.

"*Allowed?*" Uncle Monty repeated. "Of course

not! You are *implored* to come inside here, my boy. Starting first thing tomorrow morning, all of us must be here every day in preparation for the expedition to Peru. I will clear off one of those tables for you, Violet, to work on the traps. Klaus, I expect you to read all of the books about Peru that I have, and make careful notes. And Sunny can sit on the floor and bite rope. We will work all day until suppertime, and after supper we will go to the movies. Are there any objections?"

Violet, Klaus, and Sunny looked at one another and grinned. Any *objections*? The Baudelaire orphans had just been living with Count Olaf, who had made them chop wood and clean up after his drunken guests, while plotting to steal their fortune. Uncle Monty had just described a delightful way to spend one's time, and the children smiled at him eagerly. Of course there would be no objections. Violet, Klaus, and Sunny gazed at the Reptile Room and envisioned an end to their troubles as they lived their lives under Uncle Monty's care. They were wrong, of course, about their misery being over, but for the moment the three siblings were hopeful, excited, and happy.

"No, no, no," Sunny cried out, in apparent answer to Uncle Monty's question.

"Good, good, good," Uncle Monty said, smiling. "Now, let's go figure out whose room is whose."

"Uncle Monty?" Klaus asked shyly. "I just have one question."

"What is that?" Uncle Monty said.

"What's in that cage with the cloth on top of it?"

Uncle Monty looked at the cage, and then at the children. His face lit up with a smile of pure joy. "That, my dears, is a new snake which I brought over from my last journey. Gustav and myself are the only people to have seen it. Next month I will present it to the Herpetological Society as a new discovery, but in the meantime I will allow you to look at it. Gather 'round."

The Baudelaire orphans followed Uncle Monty to the cloth-covered cage, and with a flourish—the word "flourish" here means "a sweeping gesture, often used to show off"—he swooped the cloth off the cage. Inside was a large black snake, as dark as a coal mine and as thick as a sewer pipe, looking right at the orphans with shiny green eyes. With the cloth off its cage, the snake began to uncoil itself and slither around its home.

"Because I discovered it," Uncle Monty said, "I got to name it."

"What is it called?" Violet asked.

"The Incredibly Deadly Viper," Uncle Monty replied, and at that moment something happened which I'm sure will interest you. With one flick of its tail, the snake unlatched the door of its cage and slithered out onto the table, and before Uncle Monty or any of the Baudelaire orphans could say anything, it opened its mouth and bit Sunny right on the chin.

*I am* very, very sorry to leave you hanging like that, but as I was writing the tale of the Baudelaire orphans, I happened to look at the clock and realized I was running late for a formal dinner party given by a friend of mine, Madame diLustro. Madame diLustro is a good friend, an excellent detective, and a fine cook, but she flies into a rage if you arrive even five minutes later than her invitation states, so you understand that I had to dash off. You must have thought, at the end of the previous chapter, that Sunny was dead and that this was the terrible thing that happened to the Baudelaires at Uncle Monty's house, but I promise you Sunny survives this particular episode. It is Uncle Monty, unfortunately, who will be dead, but not yet.

As the fangs of the Incredibly Deadly Viper closed on Sunny's chin, Violet and Klaus watched in horror as Sunny's little eyes closed and her face grew quiet. Then, moving as suddenly as the snake, Sunny smiled brightly, opened her mouth, and bit the Incredibly Deadly Viper right on its tiny, scaled nose. The snake let go of her chin, and Violet and Klaus could see that it had left barely a mark. The two older Baudelaire siblings looked at Uncle Monty, and Uncle Monty looked back at them and laughed. His loud laughter bounced off the glass walls of the Reptile Room.

"Uncle Monty, what can we do?" Klaus said in despair.

"Oh, I'm sorry, my dears," Uncle Monty said, wiping his eyes with his hands. "You must be very frightened. But the Incredibly Deadly Viper is one of the *least* dangerous and most friendly creatures in the animal kingdom. Sunny has nothing to worry about, and neither do you."

Klaus looked at his baby sister, who was still in his arms, as she playfully gave the Incredibly Deadly Viper a big hug around its thick body, and he realized Uncle Monty must be telling the truth. "But then why is it called the Incredibly Deadly Viper?"

Uncle Monty laughed again. "It's a misnomer," he said, using a word which here means "a very wrong name." "Because I discovered it, I got to name it, remember? Don't tell anyone about the Incredibly Deadly Viper, because I'm going to present it to the Herpetological Society and give them a good scare before explaining that the snake is completely harmless! Lord knows they've teased me many times, because of my name. 'Hello hello, Montgomery Montgomery,' they say. 'How are you how are you, Montgomery Montgomery?' But at this year's conference I'm going to get back at them with this prank." Uncle Monty drew himself up to his full height and began talking in a silly, scientific voice. "'Colleagues,' I'll say, 'I would like to introduce to you a new species, the Incredibly Deadly Viper, which I found in the southwest forest of—my God! It's escaped!' And then, when all my fellow herpetologists have jumped up on chairs and tables and are shrieking in fear, I'll tell them that the snake wouldn't hurt a fly! Won't that be hysterical?"

Violet and Klaus looked at each other, and then began laughing, half in relief that their sister was unharmed, and half with amusement, because they thought Uncle Monty's prank was a good one.

Klaus put Sunny down on the floor, and the Incredibly Deadly Viper followed, wriggling its tail affectionately around Sunny, the way you might put your arm around someone of whom you were fond.

"Are there any snakes in this room that *are* dangerous?" Violet asked.

"Of course," Uncle Monty said. "You can't study snakes for forty years without encountering some dangerous ones. I have a whole cabinet of venom samples from every poisonous snake known to people, so I can study the ways in which these dangerous snakes work. There is a snake in this room whose venom is so deadly that your heart would stop before you even knew he'd bitten you. There is a snake who can open her mouth so wide she could swallow all of us, together, in one gulp. There is a pair of snakes who have learned to drive a car so recklessly that they would run you over in the street and never stop to apologize. But all of these snakes are in cages with much sturdier locks, and all of them can be handled safely when one has studied them enough. I promise that if you take time to learn the facts, no harm will come to you here in the Reptile Room."

There is a type of situation, which occurs all too often and which is occurring at this point in the story of the Baudelaire orphans, called "dramatic irony." Simply put, dramatic irony is when a person makes a harmless remark, and someone else who hears it knows something that makes the remark have a different, and usually unpleasant, meaning. For instance, if you were in a restaurant and said out loud, "I can't wait to eat the veal marsala I ordered," and there were people around who knew that the veal marsala was poisoned and that you would die as soon as you took a bite, your situation would be one of dramatic irony. Dramatic irony is a cruel occurrence, one that is almost always upsetting, and I'm sorry to have it appear in this story, but Violet, Klaus, and Sunny have such unfortunate lives that it was only a matter of time before dramatic irony would rear its ugly head.

As you and I listen to Uncle Monty tell the three Baudelaire orphans that no harm will ever come to them in the Reptile Room, we should be experiencing the strange feeling that accompanies the arrival of dramatic irony. This feeling is not unlike the sinking in one's stomach when one is in an elevator that suddenly goes down, or when you are snug in bed and your closet door suddenly creaks open to reveal the person who has been hiding there. For no matter how safe and happy the three children felt, no matter how comforting Uncle Monty's words were, you and I know that soon Uncle Monty will be dead and the Baudelaires will be miserable once again.

During the week that followed, however, the Baudelaires had a wonderful time in their new home. Each morning, they woke up and dressed in the privacy of their very own rooms, which they had chosen and decorated to their liking. Violet had chosen a room that had an enormous window looking out onto the snake-shaped hedges on the front lawn. She thought such a view might inspire her when she was inventing things. Uncle Monty had allowed her to tack up large pieces of white paper on each wall, so she could sketch out her ideas, even if they came to her in the middle of the night. Klaus had chosen a room with a cozy alcove in it—the word "alcove" here means "a very, very small nook just perfect for sitting and reading." With Uncle Monty's permission, he had carried up a large cushioned chair from the living room and placed it right in the alcove, under a heavy brass reading lamp. Each night, rather than reading in bed, he would curl himself in the chair with a book from Uncle Monty's library, sometimes until morning. Sunny had chosen a room right between Violet's and Klaus's, and filled it with small, hard objects from all over the house, so she could bite them when she felt like it. There were also assorted toys for the Incredibly Deadly Viper so the two of them could play together whenever they wanted, within reason.

But where the Baudelaire orphans most liked to be was the Reptile Room. Each morning, after breakfast, they would join Uncle Monty, who would have already started work on the upcoming expedition. Violet sat at a table with the ropes, gears, and cages that made up the different snake traps, learning how they worked, repairing them if they were broken, and occasionally making improvements to make the traps more comfortable for the snakes on their long journey from Peru to Uncle Monty's house. Klaus sat nearby, reading the books on Peru Uncle Monty had and taking notes on a pad of paper so they could refer to them later. And Sunny sat on the floor, biting a long rope into shorter pieces with great enthusiasm. But what the Baudelaire youngsters liked best was learning all about the reptiles from Uncle Monty. As they worked, he would show them the Alaskan Cow Lizard, a long green creature that produced delicious milk. They met the Dissonant Toad, which could imitate human speech in a gravelly voice. Uncle Monty taught them how to handle the Inky Newt without getting its black dye all over their fingers, and how to tell when the Irascible Python was grumpy and best left alone. He taught them not to give the Green Gimlet Toad too much water, and to never, under any circumstances, let the Virginian Wolfsnake near a typewriter.

While he was telling them about the different reptiles, Uncle Monty would often segue— a word which here means "let the conversation veer off"—to stories from his travels, describing the men, snakes, women, toads, children, and lizards he'd met on his journeys. And before too long, the Baudelaire orphans were telling Uncle Monty all about their own lives, eventually talking about their parents and how much they missed them. Uncle Monty was as interested in the Baudelaires' stories as they were in his, and sometimes they got to talking so long they scarcely had time to gobble down dinner before cramming themselves into Uncle Monty's tiny jeep and heading to the movies.

One morning, however, when the three children finished their breakfast and went into the Reptile Room, they found not Uncle Monty, but a note from him. The note read as follows:

*Dear Bambini,*

I have gone into town to buy a few last things we need for the expedition: Peruvian wasp repellent, toothbrushes, canned peaches, and a fireproof canoe. It will take a while to find the peaches, so don't expect me back until dinnertime.

Stephano, Gustav's replacement, will arrive today by taxi. Please make him feel welcome. As you know, it is only two days until the expedition, so please work very hard today.

*Your giddy uncle,*
Monty

"What does 'giddy' mean?" Violet asked, when they had finished reading the note.

"'Dizzy and excited,'" Klaus said, having learned the word from a collection of poetry he'd read in first grade. "I guess he means excited about Peru. Or maybe he's excited about having a new assistant."

"Or maybe he's excited about us," Violet said.

"Kindal!" Sunny shrieked, which probably meant "Or maybe he's excited about all these things."

"I'm a little giddy myself," Klaus said. "It's really fun to live with Uncle Monty."

"It certainly is," Violet agreed. "After the fire, I thought I would never be happy again. But our time here has been wonderful."

"I still miss our parents, though," Klaus said. "No matter how nice Uncle Monty is, I wish we still lived in our real home."

"Of course," Violet said quickly. She paused, and slowly said out loud something she had been thinking about for the past few days. "I think we'll always miss our parents. But I think we can miss them without being miserable all the time. After all, they wouldn't want us to be miserable."

"Remember that time," Klaus said wistfully, "when we were bored one rainy afternoon, and all of us painted our toenails bright red?"

"Yes," Violet said, grinning, "and I spilled some on the yellow chair."

"Archo!" Sunny said quietly, which probably meant something like "And the stain never really came out." The Baudelaire orphans smiled at each other and, without a word, began to do the day's work. For the rest of the morning they worked quietly and steadily, realizing that their contentment here at Uncle Monty's house did not erase their parents' death, not at all, but at least it made them feel better after feeling so sad, for so long.

It is unfortunate, of course, that this quiet happy moment was the last one the children would have for quite some time, but there is nothing anyone can do about it now. Just when the Baudelaires were beginning to think about lunch, they heard a car pull up in front of the house and toot its horn. To the children it signaled the arrival of Stephano. To us it should signal the beginning of more misery.

"I expect that's the new assistant," Klaus said, looking up from *The Big Peruvian Book of Small Peruvian Snakes*. "I hope he's as nice as Monty."

"Me too," Violet said, opening and shutting a toad trap to make sure it worked smoothly. "It would be unpleasant to travel to Peru with somebody who was boring or mean."

"Gerja!" Sunny shrieked, which probably meant something like "Well, let's go find out what Stephano is like!"

The Baudelaires left the Reptile Room and walked out the front door to find a taxi parked next to the snake-shaped hedges. A very tall, thin man with a long beard and no eyebrows over his eyes was getting out of the backseat, carrying a black suitcase with a shiny silver padlock.

"I'm not going to give you a tip," the bearded man was saying to the driver of the taxi, "because you talk too much. Not everybody wants to hear about your new baby, you know. Oh, hello there. I am Stephano, Dr. Montgomery's new assistant. How do you do?"

"How do you do?" Violet said, and as she approached him, there was something about his wheezy voice that seemed vaguely familiar.

"How do you do?" Klaus said, and as he looked up at Stephano, there was something about his shiny eyes that seemed quite familiar.

"Hooda!" Sunny shrieked. Stephano wasn't wearing any socks, and Sunny, crawling on the ground, could see his bare ankle between his pant cuff and his shoe. There on his ankle was something that was most familiar of all.

The Baudelaire orphans all realized the same thing at the same time, and took a step back as you might from a growling dog. This man wasn't Stephano, no matter what he called himself. The three children looked at Uncle Monty's new assistant from head to toe and saw that he was none other than Count Olaf. He may have shaved off his one long eyebrow, and grown a beard over his scraggly chin, but there was no way he could hide the tattoo of an eye on his ankle.

## CHAPTER Four

*One* of the most difficult things to think about in life is one's regrets. Something will happen to you, and you will do the wrong thing, and for years afterward you will wish you had done something different. For instance, sometimes when I am walking along the seashore, or visiting the grave of a friend, I will remember a day, a long time ago, when I didn't bring a flashlight with me to a place where I should have brought a flashlight, and the results were disastrous. *Why didn't I bring a flashlight?* I think to myself, even though it is too late to do anything about it. *I should have brought a flashlight.*

For years after this moment in the lives of the Baudelaire orphans, Klaus thought of the time when he and his siblings realized that Stephano was actually Count Olaf, and was filled with regret that he didn't call out to the driver of the taxicab who was beginning to drive back down the driveway. *Stop!* Klaus would think to himself, even though it was too late to do anything about it. *Stop! Take this man away!* Of course, it is perfectly understandable that Klaus and his sisters were too surprised to act so quickly, but Klaus would lie awake in bed, years later, thinking that maybe, just maybe, if he had acted in time, he could have saved Uncle Monty's life.

But he didn't. As the Baudelaire orphans stared at Count Olaf, the taxi drove back down the driveway and the children were alone with their nemesis, a word which here means "the worst enemy you could imagine." Olaf smiled at them the way Uncle Monty's Mongolian Meansnake would smile when a white mouse was placed in its cage each day for dinner. "Perhaps one of you might carry my suitcase into my room," he suggested in his wheezy voice. "The ride along that smelly road was dull and unpleasant and I am very tired."

"If anyone ever deserved to travel along Lousy Lane," Violet said, glaring at him, "it is you, Count Olaf. We will certainly not help you with your luggage, because we will not let you in this house."

Olaf frowned at the orphans, and then looked this way and that as if he expected to see someone hiding behind the snake-shaped hedges. "Who is Count Olaf?" he asked quizzically. "My name is Stephano. I am here to assist Montgomery Montgomery with his upcoming expedition to Peru. I assume you three are midgets who work as servants in the Montgomery home."

"We are not midgets," Klaus said sternly. "We are children. And you are not Stephano. You are Count Olaf. You may have grown a beard and shaved your eyebrow, but you are still the same despicable person and we will not let you in this house."

"Futa!" Sunny shrieked, which probably meant something like "I agree!"

Count Olaf looked at each of the Baudelaire orphans, his eyes shining brightly as if he were telling a joke. "I don't know what you're talk-ing about," he said, "but if I did, and I were this Count Olaf you speak of, I would think that you were being very rude. And if I thought you were rude, I might get angry. And if I got angry, who knows what I would do?"

The children watched as Count Olaf raised his scrawny arms in a sort of shrug. It probably isn't necessary to remind you just how violent he could be, but it certainly wasn't necessary at all to remind the Baudelaires. Klaus could still feel the bruise on his face from the time Count Olaf had struck him, when they were living in his house. Sunny still ached from being stuffed into a birdcage and dangled from the tower where he made his evil plans. And while Violet had not been the victim of any physical violence from this terrible man, she had almost been forced to marry him, and that was enough to make her pick up his suitcase and drag it slowly toward the door to the house.

"Higher," Olaf said. "Lift it higher. I don't want it dragged along the ground like that."

Klaus and Sunny hurried to help Violet with the suitcase, but even with the three of them carrying it the weight made them stagger. It was misery enough that Count Olaf had reappeared in their lives, just when they were feeling so comfortable and safe with Uncle Monty. But to actually be helping this awful person enter their home was almost more than they could bear. Olaf followed closely behind them and the three children could smell his stale breath as they brought the suitcase indoors and set it on the carpet beneath the painting of the entwined snakes.

"Thank you, orphans," Olaf said, shutting the front door behind him. "Now, Dr. Montgomery said my room would be waiting upstairs. I suppose I can carry my luggage from here. Now run along. We'll have lots of time to get to know one another later."

"We already know you, Count Olaf," Violet said. "You obviously haven't changed a bit."

"You haven't changed, either," Olaf said. "It is clear to me, Violet, that you are as stubborn as ever. And Klaus, you are still wearing those idiotic glasses from reading too many books. And I see that little Sunny here still has nine toes instead of ten."

"Fut!" Sunny shrieked, which probably meant something like "I do not!"

"What are you talking about?" Klaus said

impatiently. "She has ten toes, just like every-body else."

"Really?" Olaf said. "That's odd. I remember that she lost one of her toes in an accident." His eyes shone even brighter, as if he were telling a joke, and he reached into the pocket of his shabby coat and brought out a long knife, such as one might use for slicing bread. "I seem to recall there was a man who was so confused by being called repeatedly by the wrong name that he accidentally dropped a knife on her little foot and severed one of her toes."

Violet and Klaus looked at Count Olaf, and then at the bare foot of their little sister. "You wouldn't dare," Klaus said.

"Let's not discuss what I would or would not dare to do," Olaf said. "Let us discuss, rather, what I am to be called for as long as we are together in this house."

"We'll call you Stephano, if you insist on threatening us," Violet said, "but we won't be together in this house for long."

Stephano opened his mouth to say something, but Violet was not interested in continuing the conversation. She turned on her heel and marched primly through the enormous door of the Reptile Room, followed by her siblings. If you or I had been there, we would have thought that the Baudelaire orphans weren't scared at all, speaking so bravely like that to Stephano and then simply walking away, but once the children reached the far end of the room, their true emotions showed clearly on their faces. The Baudelaires were terrified. Violet put her hands over her face and leaned against one of the reptile cages. Klaus sank into a chair, trembling so hard that his feet rattled against the marble floor. And Sunny curled up into a little ball on the floor, so tiny you might have missed her if you walked into the room. For several moments, none of the children spoke, just listened to the muffled sounds of Stephano walking up the stairs and their own heartbeats pounding in their ears.

"How did he find us?" Klaus asked. His voice was a hoarse whisper, as if he had a sore throat. "How did he get to be Uncle Monty's assistant? What is he doing here?"

"He vowed that he'd get his hands on the Baudelaire fortune," Violet said, taking her hands away from her face and picking up Sunny, who was shivering. "That was the last thing he said to me before he escaped. He said he'd get our fortune if it was the last thing he ever did." Violet shuddered, and did not add that he'd also said that once he got their fortune, he'd do away with all three of the Baudelaire siblings. She did not need to add it. Violet, Klaus, and Sunny all knew that if he figured out a way to seize their fortune, he would slit the throats of the Baudelaire orphans as easily as you or I might eat a small butter cookie.

"What can we do?" Klaus asked. "Uncle Monty won't be back for hours."

"Maybe we can call Mr. Poe," Violet said. "It's the middle of business hours, but maybe he could leave the bank for an emergency."

"He wouldn't believe us," Klaus said. "Remember when we tried to tell him about Count Olaf when we lived there? He took such a long time to realize the truth, it was almost too late. I think we should run away. If we leave right now, we could probably get to town in time to catch a train far away from here."

Violet pictured the three of them, all alone, walking along Lousy Lane beneath the sour apple trees, with the bitter smell of horseradish encircling them. "Where would we go?" she asked.

"Anywhere," Klaus said. "Anywhere but here. We could go far away where Count Olaf wouldn't find us, and change our names so no one would know who we were."

"We haven't any money," Violet pointed out. "How could we live by ourselves?"

"We could get jobs," Klaus replied. "I could work in a library, maybe, and you could work in some sort of mechanical factory. Sunny probably couldn't get a job at her age, but in a few years she could."

The three orphans were quiet. They tried to picture leaving Uncle Monty and living by themselves, trying to find jobs and take care of each other. It was a very lonely prospect. The Baudelaire children sat in sad silence awhile, and they were each thinking the same thing: They wished that their parents had never been killed in the fire, and that their lives had never been turned topsy-turvy the way they had. If only the Baudelaire parents were still alive, the youngsters wouldn't even have heard of Count Olaf, let alone have him settling into their home and undoubtedly making evil plans.

"We can't leave," Violet said finally. "Count Olaf found us once, and I'm sure he'd find us again, no matter how far we went. Plus, who knows where Count Olaf's assistants are? Perhaps they've surrounded the house right now, keeping watch in case we're on to him."

Klaus shivered. He hadn't been thinking of

Olaf's assistants. Besides scheming to get his hands on the Baudelaire fortune, Olaf was the leader of a terrible theater troupe, and his fellow actors were always ready to help him with his plans. They were a gruesome crew, each more terrifying than the next. There was a bald man with a long nose, who always wore a black robe. There were two women who always had ghostly white powder on their faces. There was a person so large and blank-looking that you couldn't tell if it was a man or a woman. And there was a skinny man with two hooks where his hands should have been. Violet was right. Any of these people could be lurking outside Uncle Monty's house, waiting to catch them if they tried to escape.

"I think we should just wait for Uncle Monty to come back, and tell him what has happened," Violet said. "He'll believe us. If we tell him about the tattoo, he'll at least ask *Stephano* for an explanation." Violet's tone of voice when she said "Stephano" indicated her utter scorn for Olaf's disguise.

"Are you sure?" Klaus said. "After all, Uncle Monty is the one who hired *Stephano*." Klaus's tone of voice when *he* said "Stephano" indicated that he shared his sister's feelings. "For all we know, Uncle Monty and Stephano have planned something together."

"Minda!" Sunny shrieked, which probably meant something like "Don't be ridiculous, Klaus!"

Violet shook her head. "Sunny's right. I can't believe that Uncle Monty would be in cahoots with Olaf. He's been so kind and generous to us, and besides, if they were working together, Olaf wouldn't insist on using a different name."

"That's true," Klaus said thoughtfully. "So we wait for Uncle Monty."

"We wait," Violet agreed.

"Tojoo," Sunny said solemnly, and the siblings looked at one another glumly. Waiting is one of life's hardships. It is hard enough to wait for chocolate cream pie while burnt roast beef is still on your plate. It is plenty difficult to wait for Halloween when the tedious month of September is still ahead of you. But to wait for one's adopted uncle to come home while a greedy and violent man is upstairs was one of the worst waits the Baudelaires had ever experienced. To get their mind off it, they tried to continue with their work, but the children were too anxious to get anything done. Violet tried to fix a hinged door on one of the traps, but all she could concentrate on was the knot of worry in her stomach. Klaus tried to read about protecting oneself from thorny Peruvian plants, but thoughts of Stephano kept clouding his brain. And Sunny tried to bite rope, but she had a cold chill of fear running through her teeth and she soon gave up. She didn't even feel like playing with the Incredibly Deadly Viper. So the Baudelaires spent the rest of the afternoon sitting silently in the Reptile Room, looking out the window for Uncle Monty's jeep and listening to the occasional noise from upstairs. They didn't even want to think about what Stephano might be unpacking.

Finally, as the snake-shaped hedges began to cast long, skinny shadows in the setting sun, the three children heard an approaching engine, and the jeep pulled up. A large canoe was strapped to the roof of the jeep, and the backseat was piled with Monty's purchases. Uncle Monty got out, struggling under the weight of several shopping bags, and saw the children through the glass walls of the Reptile Room. He smiled at them. They smiled back, and in that instant when they smiled was created another moment of regret for them. Had they not paused to smile at Monty but instead gone dashing out to the car, they might have had a brief moment alone with him. But by the time they reached the entry hall, he was already talking to Stephano.

"I didn't know what kind of toothbrush you preferred," Uncle Monty was saying apologetically, "so I got you one with extra-firm bristles because that's the kind I like. Peruvian food tends to be sticky, so you need to have at least one extra toothbrush whenever you go there."

"Extra-firm bristles are fine with me," Stephano said, speaking to Uncle Monty but looking at the orphans with his shiny, shiny eyes. "Shall I carry in the canoe?"

"Yes, but my goodness, you can't carry it all by yourself," Uncle Monty said. "Klaus, please help Stephano, will you?"

"Uncle Monty," Violet said, "we have something very important to tell you."

"I'm all ears," Uncle Monty said, "but first let me show you the wasp repellent I picked up. I'm so glad Klaus read up on the insect situation in Peru, because the other repellents I have would have been no use at all." Uncle Monty rooted through one of the bags on his arm as the children waited impatiently for him to finish. "This one contains a chemical called—"

"Uncle Monty," Klaus said, "what we have to tell you really can't wait."

"Klaus," Uncle Monty said, his eyebrows rising in surprise, "it's not polite to interrupt when your uncle is talking. Now, please help Stephano with the canoe, and we'll talk about anything you want in a few moments."

Klaus sighed, but followed Stephano out the open door. Violet watched them walking toward the jeep as Uncle Monty put down the shopping bags and faced her. "I can't remember what I was saying about the repellent," he said, a little crossly. "I hate losing my train of thought."

"What we have to tell you," Violet began, but she stopped when something caught her eye. Monty was facing away from the door, so he couldn't see what Stephano was doing, but Violet saw Stephano stop at the snake-shaped hedges, reach into his coat pocket, and take out the long knife. Its blade caught the light of the setting sun and it glowed brightly, like a lighthouse. As you probably know, lighthouses serve as warning signals, telling ships where the shore is so they don't run into it. The shining knife was a warning, too.

Klaus looked at the knife, and then at Stephano, and then at Violet. Violet looked at Klaus, and then at Stephano, and then at Monty. Sunny looked at everyone. Only Monty didn't notice what was going on, so intent was he on remembering whatever he was babbling about wasp repellent. "What we have to tell you," Violet began again, but she couldn't continue. Stephano didn't say a word. He didn't have to. Violet knew that if she breathed one word about his true identity, Stephano would hurt her brother, right there at the snake-shaped hedges. Without saying a word, the nemesis of the Baudelaire orphans had sent a very clear warning.

## CHAPTER Five

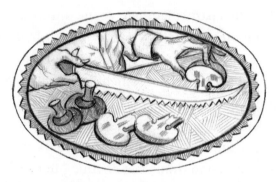

*That* night felt like the longest and most terrible the Baudelaire orphans had ever had, and they'd had plenty. There was one night, shortly after Sunny was born, that all three children had a horrible flu, and tossed and turned in the grasp of a terrible fever, while their father tried to soothe them all at once, placing cold washcloths on their sweaty brows. The night after their parents had been killed, the three children had stayed at Mr. Poe's house, and had stayed up all night, too miserable and confused to even try to sleep. And of course, they had spent many a long and terrible night while living with Count Olaf.

But this particular night seemed worse. From the moment of Monty's arrival until bedtime, Stephano kept the children under his constant surveillance, a phrase which here means "kept watching them so they couldn't possibly talk to Uncle Monty alone and reveal that he was really Count Olaf," and Uncle Monty was too preoccupied to think that anything unusual was going on. When they brought in the rest of Uncle Monty's purchases, Stephano carried bags with only one hand, keeping the other one in his coat pocket where the long knife was hidden, but Uncle Monty was too excited about all the new supplies to ask about it. When they went into the kitchen to prepare dinner, Stephano smiled menacingly at the children as he sliced mushrooms, but Uncle Monty was too busy making sure the stroganoff sauce didn't boil to even notice that Stephano was using his own threatening knife for the chopping. Over dinner, Stephano told funny stories and praised Monty's scientific work, and Uncle Monty was so flattered he didn't even think to guess that Stephano was holding a knife under the table, rubbing the blade gently against Violet's knee for the entire meal. And when Uncle Monty announced that he would spend the evening showing his new assistant around the Reptile Room, he was too eager to realize that the Baudelaires simply went up to bed without a word.

For the first time, having individual bedrooms seemed like a hardship rather than a luxury, for without one another's company the orphans felt even more lonely and helpless. Violet stared at the paper tacked to her wall and tried to imagine what Stephano was planning. Klaus sat in his large cushioned chair and turned on his brass reading lamp but was too worried to even open a book. Sunny stared at her hard objects but didn't bite a single one of them.

All three children thought of walking down the hall to Uncle Monty's room and waking him up to tell him what was wrong. But to get to his bedroom, they would have to walk past the room in which Stephano was staying, and all night long Stephano kept watch in a chair placed in front of his open door. When the orphans opened their doors to peer down the dark hallway, they saw Stephano's pale, shaved head, which seemed to be floating above his body in the darkness. And they could see his knife, which Stephano was moving slowly like the pendulum of a grandfather clock. Back and forth it went, back and forth, glinting in the dim light, and the sight was so fearsome they didn't dare try walking down the hallway.

Finally, the light in the house turned the pale blue-gray of early dawn, and the Baudelaire children walked blearily down the stairs to breakfast, tired and achy from their sleepless night. They sat around the table where they had eaten cake on their first morning at the house, and picked listlessly at their food. For the first time since their arrival at Uncle Monty's, they were not eager to enter the Reptile Room and begin the day's work.

"I suppose we have to go in now," Violet said finally, putting aside her scarcely nibbled toast. "I'm sure Uncle Monty has already started working, and is expecting us."

"And I'm sure that Stephano is there, too," Klaus said, staring glumly into his cereal bowl. "We'll never get a chance to tell Uncle Monty what we know about him."

"Yinga," Sunny said sadly, dropping her untouched raw carrot to the floor.

"If only Uncle Monty knew what we know," Violet said, "and Stephano knew that he knew what we know. But Uncle Monty doesn't know what we know, and Stephano knows that he doesn't know what we know."

"I know," Klaus said.

"I know you know," Violet said, "but what we don't know is what Count Olaf—I mean *Stephano*—is really up to. He's after our fortune, certainly, but how can he get it if we're under Uncle Monty's care?"

"Maybe he's just going to wait until you're of age, and then steal the fortune," Klaus said.

"Four years is a long time to wait," Violet said. The three orphans were quiet, as each remembered where they had been four years ago. Violet had been ten, and had worn her hair very short. She remembered that sometime around her tenth birthday she had invented a new kind of pencil sharpener. Klaus had been about eight, and he remembered how interested he had been in comets, reading all the astronomy books his parents had in their library. Sunny, of course, had not been born four years ago, and she sat and tried to remember what that was like. Very dark, she thought, with nothing to bite. For all three youngsters, four years did seem like a very long time.

"Come on, come on, you are moving very slowly this morning," Uncle Monty said, bursting into the room. His face seemed even brighter than usual, and he was holding a small bunch of folded papers in one hand. "Stephano has only worked here one day, and he's already in the Reptile Room. In fact, he was up before I was—I ran into him on my way down the stairs. He's an eager beaver. But you three—you're moving like the Hungarian Sloth Snake, whose top speed is half an inch per hour! We have lots to do today, and I'd like to catch the six o'clock showing of *Zombies in the Snow* tonight, so let's try to hurry, hurry, hurry."

Violet looked at Uncle Monty, and realized that this might be their only opportunity to talk to him alone, without Stephano around, but he seemed so wound up they weren't sure if he would listen to them. "Speaking of Stephano," she said timidly, "we'd like to talk to you about him."

Uncle Monty's eyes widened, and he looked

around him as if there were spies in the room before leaning in to whisper to the children. "I'd like to talk to you, too," he said. "I have my suspicions about Stephano, and I'd like to discuss them with you."

The Baudelaire orphans looked at one another in relief. "You do?" Klaus said.

"Of course," Uncle Monty said. "Last night I began to get very suspicious about this new assistant of mine. There's something a little spooky about him, and I—" Uncle Monty looked around again, and began speaking even softer, so the children had to hold their breaths to hear him. "And I think we should discuss it outside. Shall we?"

The children nodded in agreement, and rose from the table. Leaving their dirty breakfast dishes behind, which is not a good thing to do in general but perfectly acceptable in the face of an emergency, they walked with Uncle Monty to the front entryway, past the painting of two snakes entwined together, out the front door, and onto the lawn, as if they wanted to talk to the snake-shaped hedges instead of to one another.

"I don't mean to be vainglorious," Uncle Monty began, using a word which here means "braggy," "but I really am one of the most widely respected herpetologists in the world."

Klaus blinked. It was an unexpected beginning for the conversation. "Of course you are," he said, "but—"

"And because of this, I'm sad to say," Uncle Monty continued, as if he had not heard, "many people are jealous of me."

"I'm sure that's true," Violet said, puzzled.

"And when people are jealous," Uncle Monty said, shaking his head, "they will do anything. They will do crazy things. When I was getting my herpetology degree, my roommate was so envious of a new toad I had discovered that he stole and ate my only specimen. I had to X-ray his stomach, and use the X-rays rather than the toad in my presentation. And something tells me we may have a similar situation here."

What was Uncle Monty talking about?

"I'm afraid I don't quite follow you," Klaus said, which is the polite way of saying "What are you talking about, Uncle Monty?"

"Last night, after you went to bed, Stephano asked me a few too many questions about all the snakes and about my upcoming expedition. And do you know why?"

"I think so," Violet began, but Uncle Monty interrupted her.

"It is because this man who is calling himself Stephano," he said, "is really a member of the Herpetological Society, and he is here to try and find the Incredibly Deadly Viper so he can pre-empt my presentation. Do you three know what the word 'preempt' means?"

"No," Violet said, "but—"

"It means that I think this Stephano is going to steal my snake," Uncle Monty said, "and present it to the Herpetological Society. Because it is a new species, there's no way I can prove I discovered it. Before we know it, the Incredibly Deadly Viper will be called the Stephano Snake, or something dreadful like that. And if he's planning that, just think what he will do to our Peruvian expedition. Each toad we catch, each venom sample we put into a test tube, each snake interview we record—every scrap of work we do—will fall into the hands of this Herpetological Society spy."

"He's not a Herpetological Society spy," Klaus said impatiently, "he's Count Olaf!"

"I know just what you mean!" Uncle Monty said excitedly. "This sort of behavior is indeed as dastardly as that terrible man's. That is why I'm doing this." He raised one hand and waved the folded papers in the air. "As you know," he said, "tomorrow we are leaving for Peru. These are our tickets for the five o'clock voyage on the *Prospero*, a fine ship that will take us across the sea to South America. There's a ticket for me, one for Violet, one for Klaus, one for Stephano, but not one for Sunny because we're going to hide her in a suitcase to save money."

"Deepo!"

"I'm kidding about that. But I'm not kidding about this." Uncle Monty, his face flushed with excitement, took one of the folded papers and began ripping it into tiny pieces. "This is Stephano's ticket. He's not going to Peru with us after all. Tomorrow morning, I'm going to tell him that he needs to stay here and look after my specimens instead. That way we can run a successful expedition in peace."

"But Uncle Monty—" Klaus said.

"How many times must I remind you it's not polite to interrupt?" Uncle Monty interrupted, shaking his head. "In any case, I know what you're worried about. You're worried what will happen if he stays here alone with the Incredibly Deadly Viper. But don't worry. The Viper will join us on the expedition, traveling in one of our snake carrying cases. I don't know why you're looking so glum, Sunny. I thought you'd be happy to have the Viper's company. So don't look so worried, bambini. As you can see, your Uncle Monty has the situation in hand."

When somebody is a little bit wrong—say, when a waiter puts nonfat milk in your espresso macchiato, instead of lowfat milk—it is often quite easy to explain to them how and why they are wrong. But if somebody is surpassingly wrong—say, when a waiter bites your nose instead of taking your order—you can often be so surprised that you are unable to say anything at all. Paralyzed by how wrong the waiter is, your mouth would hang slightly open and your eyes would blink over and over, but you would be unable to say a word. This is what the Baudelaire children did. Uncle Monty was so wrong about Stephano, in thinking he was a herpetological spy rather than Count Olaf, that the three siblings could scarcely think of a way to tell him so.

"Come now, my dears," Uncle Monty said. "We've wasted enough of the morning on talk. We have to—*ow!*" He interrupted himself with a cry of surprise and pain, and fell to the ground.

"Uncle Monty!" Klaus cried. The Baudelaire children saw that a large, shiny object was on top of him, and realized a moment later what the object was: it was the heavy brass reading lamp, the one standing next to the large cushioned chair in Klaus's room.

"*Ow!*" Uncle Monty said again, pulling the lamp off him. "That really hurt. My shoulder may be sprained. It's a good thing it didn't land on my head, or it really could have done some damage."

"But where did it come from?" Violet asked.

"It must have fallen from the window," Uncle Monty said, pointing up to where Klaus's room was. "Whose room is that? Klaus, I believe it is yours. You must be more careful. You can't dangle heavy objects out the window like that. Look what almost happened."

"But that lamp wasn't anywhere near my window," Klaus said. "I keep it in the alcove, so I can read in that large chair."

"Really, Klaus," Uncle Monty said, standing up and handing him the lamp. "Do you honestly expect me to believe that the lamp danced over to the window and leaped onto my shoulder? Please put this back in your room, in a safe place, and we'll say no more about it."

"But—" Klaus said, but his older sister interrupted him.

"I'll help you, Klaus," Violet said. "We'll find a place for it where it's safe."

"Well, don't be too long," Uncle Monty said, rubbing his shoulder. "We'll see you in the Reptile Room. Come, Sunny."

Walking through the entry hall, the four parted ways at the stairs, with Uncle Monty and Sunny going to the enormous door of the Reptile Room, and Violet and Klaus carrying the heavy brass lamp up to Klaus's room.

"You know *very well*," Klaus hissed to his sister, "that I was *not careless* with this lamp."

"Of course I know that," Violet whispered. "But there's no use trying to explain that to

Uncle Monty. He thinks Stephano is a herpetological spy. You know as well as I do that Stephano was responsible for this."

"How clever of you to figure that out," said a voice at the top of the stairs, and Violet and Klaus were so surprised they almost dropped the lamp. It was Stephano, or, if you prefer, it was Count Olaf. It was the bad guy. "But then, you've always been clever children," he continued. "A little too clever for my taste, but you won't be around for long, so I'm not troubled by it."

"You're not very clever yourself, " Klaus said fiercely. "This heavy brass lamp almost hit us, but if anything happens to my sisters or me, you'll never get your hands on the Baudelaire fortune."

"Dear me, dear me," Stephano said, his grimy teeth showing as he smiled. "If I wanted to harm *you*, orphan, your blood would already be pouring down these stairs like a waterfall. No, I'm not going to harm a hair on any Baudelaire head—not here in this house. You needn't be afraid of me, little ones, until we find ourselves in a location where crimes are more difficult to trace."

"And where would that be?" Violet asked. "We plan to stay right here until we grow up."

"Really?" Stephano said, in that sneaky, sneaky voice. "Why, I had the impression we were leaving the country tomorrow."

"Uncle Monty tore up your ticket," Klaus replied triumphantly. "He was suspicious of you, so he changed his plans and now you're not going with us."

Stephano's smile turned into a scowl, and his stained teeth seemed to grow bigger. His eyes grew so shiny that it hurt Violet and Klaus to look at them. "I wouldn't rely on that," he said, in a terrible, terrible voice. "Even the best plans can change if there's an accident." He pointed one spiky finger at the brass reading lamp. "And accidents happen all the time."

## CHAPTER Six

*Bad* circumstances have a way of ruining things
that would otherwise be pleasant. So it was with
the Baudelaire orphans and the movie *Zombies
in the Snow*. All afternoon, the three children had
sat and worried in the Reptile Room, under the
mocking stare of Stephano and the oblivious—
the word "oblivious"
here means "not aware
that Stephano was really
Count Olaf and thus
being in a great deal of
danger"—chatter of Uncle
Monty. So by the time it
was evening, the siblings

were in no mood for cinematic entertainment. Uncle Monty's jeep was really too small to hold him, Stephano and the three orphans, so Klaus and Violet shared a seat, and poor Sunny had to sit on Stephano's filthy lap, but the Baudelaires were too preoccupied to even notice their discomfort.

The children sat all in a row at the multiplex, with Uncle Monty to one side, while Stephano sat in the middle and hogged the popcorn. But the children were too anxious to eat any snacks, and too busy trying to figure out what Stephano planned to do to enjoy *Zombies in the Snow*, which was a fine film. When the zombies first rose out of the snowbanks surrounding the tiny Alpine fishing village, Violet tried to imagine a way in which Stephano could get aboard the *Prospero* without a ticket and accompany them to Peru. When the town fathers constructed a barrier of sturdy oak, only to have the zombies chomp their way through it, Klaus was concerned with exactly what Stephano had meant when he spoke about accidents. And when Gerta, the little milkmaid, made friends with the zombies and asked them to please stop eating the villagers, Sunny, who was of course scarcely old enough to comprehend the orphans' situation, tried to think up a way to defeat Stephano's plans, whatever they were. In the final scene of the movie, the zombies and villagers celebrated May Day together, but the three Baudelaire orphans were too nervous and afraid to enjoy themselves one bit. On the way home, Uncle Monty tried to talk to the silent, worried children sitting in the back, but they hardly said a word in reply and eventually he fell silent.

When the jeep pulled up to the snake-shaped hedges, the Baudelaire children dashed out and ran to the front door without even saying good night to their puzzled guardian. With heavy hearts they climbed the stairs to their bedrooms, but when they reached their doors they could not bear to part.

"Could we all spend the night in the same room?" Klaus asked Violet timidly. "Last night I felt as if I were in a jail cell, worrying all by myself."

"Me too," Violet admitted. "Since we're not going to sleep, we might as well not sleep in the same place."

"Tikko," Sunny agreed, and followed her siblings into Violet's room. Violet looked around the bedroom and remembered how excited she had been to move into it just a short while ago. Now, the enormous window with the view of the snake-shaped hedges seemed depressing rather than inspiring, and the blank pages tacked to her wall, rather than being convenient, seemed only to remind her of how anxious she was.

"I see you haven't worked much on your inventions," Klaus said gently. "I haven't been reading at all. When Count Olaf is around, it sure puts a damper on the imagination."

"Not always," Violet pointed out. "When we lived with him, you read all about nuptial law to find out about his plan, and I invented a grappling hook to put a stop to it."

"In this situation, though," Klaus said glumly, "we don't even know what Count Olaf is up to. How can we formulate a plan if we don't know *his* plan?"

"Well, let's try to hash this out," Violet said, using an expression which here means "talk about something at length until we completely understand it." "Count Olaf, calling himself Stephano, has come to this house in disguise and is obviously after the Baudelaire fortune."

"And," Klaus continued, "once he gets his hands on it, he plans to kill us."

"Tadu," Sunny murmured solemnly, which probably meant something along the lines of "It's a loathsome situation in which we find ourselves."

"However," Violet said, "if he harms us,

there's no way he can get to our fortune. That's why he tried to marry me last time."

"Thank God that didn't work," Klaus said, shivering. "Then Count Olaf would be my brother-in-law. But this time he's not planning to marry you. He said something about an accident."

"And about heading to a location where crimes are more difficult to trace," Violet said, remembering his words. "That must mean Peru. But Stephano isn't going to Peru. Uncle Monty tore up his ticket."

"Doog!" Sunny shrieked, in a generic cry of frustration, and pounded her little fist on the floor. The word "generic" here means "when one is unable to think of anything else to say," and Sunny was not alone in this. Violet and Klaus were of course too old to say things like "Doog!" but they wished they weren't. They wished they could figure out Count Olaf's plan. They wished their situation didn't seem as mysterious and hopeless as it did, and they wished they were young enough to simply shriek "Doog!" and pound their fists on the floor. And most of all, of course, they wished that their parents were alive and that the Baudelaires were all safe in the home where they had been born.

And as fervently as the Baudelaire orphans wished their circumstances were different, I wish that I could somehow change the circumstances of this story for you. Even as I sit here, safe as can be and so very far from Count Olaf, I can scarcely bear to write another word. Perhaps it would be best if you shut this book right now and never read the rest of this horrifying story. You can imagine, if you wish, that an hour later, the Baudelaire orphans suddenly figured out what Stephano was up to and were able to save Uncle Monty's life. You can picture the police arriving with all their flashing lights and sirens, and dragging Stephano away to jail for the rest of his life. You can pretend, even though it is not so, that the Baudelaires are living happily with Uncle Monty to this day. Or

best of all, you can conjure up the illusion that
the Baudelaire parents have not been killed,
and that the terrible fire and Count Olaf and
Uncle Monty and all the other unfortunate
events are nothing more than a dream, a figment
of the imagination.

But this story is not a happy one, and I am not
happy to tell you that the Baudelaire orphans
sat dumbly in Violet's room—the word "dumbly"
here means "without speaking," rather than "in
a stupid way"—for the rest of the night. Had
someone peeped through the bedroom window
as the morning sun rose, they would have seen
the three children huddled together on the bed,
their eyes wide open and dark with worry. But
nobody peeped through the window. Somebody
knocked on the door, four loud knocks as if
something were being nailed shut.

The children blinked and looked at one
another. "Who is it?" Klaus called out, his voice
crackly from being silent so long.

Instead of an answer, whoever it was simply

turned the knob and the door swung slowly open. There stood Stephano, with his clothes all rumpled and his eyes shining brighter than they ever had before.

"Good morning," he said. "It's time to leave for Peru. There is just room for three orphans and myself in the jeep, so get a move on."

"We told you yesterday that you weren't going," Violet said. She hoped her voice sounded braver than she felt.

"It is your Uncle Monty who isn't going," Stephano said, and raised the part of his forehead where his eyebrow should have been.

"Don't be ridiculous," Klaus said. "Uncle Monty wouldn't miss this expedition for the world."

"Ask him," Stephano said, and the Baudelaires saw a familiar expression on his face. His mouth scarcely moved, but his eyes were shining as if he'd just told a joke. "Why don't you ask him? He's down in the Reptile Room."

"We *will* ask him," Violet said. "Uncle Monty

has no intention of letting you take us to Peru alone." She rose from the bed, took the hands of her siblings, and walked quickly past Stephano who was smirking in the doorway. "We *will* ask him," Violet said again, and Stephano gave a little bow as the children walked out of the room.

The hallway was strangely quiet, and blank as the eyes of a skull. "Uncle Monty?" Violet called, at the end of the hallway. Nobody answered.

Aside from a few creaks on the steps, the whole house was eerily quiet, as if it had been deserted for many years. "Uncle Monty?" Klaus called, at the bottom of the stairs. They heard nothing.

Standing on tiptoe, Violet opened the enormous door of the Reptile Room and for a moment, the orphans stared into the room as if hypnotized, entranced by the odd blue light which the sunrise made as it shone through the glass ceiling and walls. In the dim glow, they could see only silhouettes of the various reptiles as they moved around in their cages, or slept, curled into shapeless dark masses.

Their footsteps echoing off the glimmering walls, the three siblings walked through the Reptile Room, toward the far end, where Uncle Monty's library lay waiting for them. Even though the dark room felt mysterious and strange, it was a comforting mystery, and a safe strangeness. They remembered Uncle Monty's promise: that if they took time to learn the facts, no harm would come to them here in the Reptile Room. However, you and I remember that Uncle Monty's promise was laden with dramatic irony, and now, here in the early-morning gloom of the Reptile Room, that irony was going to come to fruition, a phrase which here means "the Baudelaires were finally to learn of it." For just as they reached the books, the three siblings could see a large, shadowy mass huddled in the far corner. Nervously, Klaus switched on one of the reading lamps to get a better look.

The shadowy mass was Uncle Monty. His mouth was slightly agape, as if he were surprised, and his eyes were wide open, but he didn't appear to see them. His face, usually so rosy, was very, very pale, and under his left eye were two small holes, right in a line, the sort of mark made by the two fangs of a snake.

"Divo soom?" Sunny asked, and tugged at his pants leg. Uncle Monty did not move. As he had promised, no harm had come to the Baudelaire orphans in the Reptile Room, but great harm had come to Uncle Monty.

## CHAPTER Seven

"*My,* my, my, my, my," said a voice from behind them, and the Baudelaire orphans turned to find Stephano standing there, the black suitcase with the shiny silver padlock in his hands and a look of brummagem surprise on his face. "Brummagem" is such a rare word for "fake" that even Klaus didn't know what it meant, but the children did not have to be told that Stephano was pretending to be

surprised. "What a terrible accident has happened here. Snakebite. Whoever discovers this will be most upset."

"You—" Violet began to say, but her throat fluttered, as if the fact of Uncle Monty's death were food that tasted terrible. "You—" she said again.

Stephano took no notice. "Of course, after they discover that Dr. Montgomery is dead, they'll wonder what became of those repulsive orphans he had lying around the house. But they'll be long gone. Speaking of which, it's time to leave. The *Prospero* sails at five o'clock from Hazy Harbor and I'd like to be the first passenger aboard. That way I'll have time for a bottle of wine before lunch."

"How could you?" Klaus whispered hoarsely. He couldn't take his eyes off Uncle Monty's pale, pale face. "How could you do this? How could you murder him?"

"Why, Klaus, I'm surprised," Stephano said, and walked over to Uncle Monty's body. "A smarty-pants boy like you should be able to figure out that your chubby old uncle died from snakebite, not from murder. Look at those teeth marks. Look at his pale, pale face. Look at these staring eyes."

"*Stop it!*" Violet said. "*Don't talk like that!*"

"You're right!" Stephano said. "There's no time for chitchat! We have a ship to catch! Let's move!"

"We're not going anywhere with you," Klaus said. His face was pinched with the effort of focusing on their predicament rather than going to pieces. "We will stay here until the police come."

"And how do you suppose the police will know to come?" Stephano said.

"We will call them," Klaus said, in what he hoped was a firm tone of voice, and began to walk toward the door.

Stephano dropped his suitcase, the shiny silver padlock making a clattering sound as it hit the marble floor. He took a few steps and blocked Klaus's way, his eyes wide and red with fury. "I am *so tired*," Stephano snarled, "of having to *explain* everything to you. You're supposed to be *so very smart*, and yet you always seem to forget about *this!*" He reached into his pocket and pulled out the jagged knife. "This is my knife. It is very sharp and very eager to hurt you— almost as eager as I am. If you don't do what I say, you will suffer bodily harm. Is that clear enough for you? Now, get in the damn jeep."

It is, as you know, very, very rude and usually unnecessary to use profanity, but the Baudelaire orphans were too terrified to point this out to Stephano. Taking a last look at their poor Uncle Monty, the three children followed Stephano to the door of the Reptile Room to get in the damn jeep. To add insult to injury—a phrase which here means "forcing somebody to do an unpleasant task when they're already very upset"— Stephano forced Violet to carry his suitcase out of the house, but she was too lost in her own thoughts to care. She was remembering the last conversation she and her siblings had had with Uncle Monty, and thinking with a cold rush of shame that it hadn't really been a conversation at all. You will recall, of course, that on the ride home from seeing *Zombies in the Snow*, the children had been so worried about Stephano that they hadn't said a word to Uncle Monty, and that when the jeep had arrived at the house, the Baudelaire orphans had dashed upstairs to hash out the situation, without even saying good night to the man who now lay dead under a sheet in the Reptile Room. As the youngsters reached the jeep, Violet tried to remember if they had even thanked him for taking them to the movies, but the night was all a blur. She thought that she, Klaus, and Sunny had probably said "Thank you, Uncle Monty," when they were standing together at the ticket booth, but she couldn't be sure. Stephano opened the door of the jeep and gestured with the knife, ushering Klaus and Sunny into the tiny backseat and Violet, the black suitcase heavy on her lap, into the front seat beside him. The orphans had a brief hope that the engine would not start when Stephano turned the key in the ignition, but this was a futile hope. Uncle Monty took good care of his jeep, and it started right up.

Violet, Klaus, and Sunny looked behind them as Stephano began to drive alongside the snake-shaped hedges. At the sight of the Reptile Room, which Uncle Monty had filled so carefully with his specimens and in which he was now a sort of specimen himself, the weight of the Baudelaires' despair was too much for them and they quietly began to cry. It is a curious thing, the death of a loved one. We all know that our time in this world is limited, and that eventually all of us will end up underneath some sheet, never to wake up. And yet it is always a surprise when it happens to someone we know. It is like walking up the stairs to your bedroom in the dark, and thinking there is one more stair than there is. Your foot falls down, through the air, and there is a sickly moment of dark surprise as you try and readjust the way you thought of things. The Baudelaire orphans were crying not only for their Uncle Monty, but for their own parents, and this dark and curious feeling of falling that accompanies any great loss.

What was to happen to them? Stephano had heartlessly slaughtered the man who was supposed to be watching over the Baudelaires, and now they were all alone. What would Stephano do to them? He was supposed to be left behind when they went to Peru, and now he would be leaving with them on the *Prospero*. And what terrible things would happen in Peru? Would anybody rescue them there? Would Stephano get his hands on the fortune? And what would happen to the three children afterward? These are frightening questions, and if you are thinking about such matters, they require your full attention, and the orphans were so immersed in thinking about them that they didn't realize that Stephano was about to collide with another automobile until the moment of impact.

There was a horrible tearing sound of metal and glass as a black car crashed into Uncle Monty's jeep, throwing the children to the floor with a jarring *thump* that felt as though it left the Baudelaire stomachs up on the seat. The black suitcase lurched into Violet's shoulder and then forward into the windshield, which immediately cracked in a dozen places so it looked like a spiderweb. Stephano gave a cry of surprise and turned the steering wheel this way and that, but the two vehicles were locked together and, with another *thump*, veered off the road into a small pile of mud. It is a rare occurrence when a car accident can be called a stroke of good fortune, but that was most certainly the case here. With the snake-shaped hedges still clearly visible behind them, the Baudelaires' journey toward Hazy Harbor had stopped.

Stephano gave another sharp cry, this one of rage. "Blasted furnaces of hell!" he shouted, as Violet rubbed her shoulder to make sure she wasn't seriously hurt. Klaus and Sunny got up cautiously from the jeep floor and looked out the cracked windshield. There appeared to be only one person in the other car, but it was hard to tell, as that vehicle had clearly suffered much more damage than Monty's jeep. Its entire front had pleated itself together, like an accordion, and one hubcap was spinning noisily on the pavement of Lousy Lane, making blurry circles as if it were a giant coin somebody had dropped. The driver was dressed in gray and making a rough hacking sound as he opened the crumpled door of the car and struggled his way out. He made the hacking sound again, and then reached into a pocket of his suit and pulled out a white handkerchief.

"It's Mr. Poe!" Klaus cried.

It *was* Mr. Poe, coughing away as usual, and the children were so delighted to see him that they found themselves smiling despite their horrible circumstances. "Mr. Poe! Mr. Poe!" Violet cried, reaching around Stephano's suitcase to open the passenger door.

Stephano reached out an arm and grabbed her sore shoulder, turning his head slowly so that each child saw his shiny eyes. "This changes *nothing*!" he hissed at them. "This is a bit of luck for you, but it is your last. The three of you will be back in this car with me and heading toward Hazy Harbor in time to catch the *Prospero*, I promise you."

"We'll see about that," Violet replied, opening the door and sliding out from beneath the suitcase. Klaus opened his door and followed her, carrying Sunny. "Mr. Poe! Mr. Poe!"

"Violet?" Mr. Poe asked. "Violet Baudelaire? Is that you?"

"Yes, Mr. Poe," Violet said. "It's all of us, and we're so grateful you ran into us like this."

"Well, I wouldn't say that," Mr. Poe said. "This was clearly the other driver's fault. *You* ran into *me*."

"How dare you!" Stephano shouted, and got out of the car himself, wrinkling his nose at the smell of horseradish that filled the air. He stomped over to where Mr. Poe was standing, but halfway there the children saw his face change from one of pure rage to one of brummagem confusion and sadness. "I'm sorry," he said, in a high, fluttery voice. "This whole thing is my fault. I'm so distressed by what has happened that I wasn't paying any attention to the rules of the road. I hope you're not hurt, Mr. Foe."

"It's *Poe*," Mr. Poe said. "My name is *Poe*. I'm not hurt. Luckily, it looks like nobody was hurt. I wish the same could be said for my car. But who are you and what are you doing with the Baudelaire children?"

"I'll tell you who he is," Klaus said. "He's—"

"Please, Klaus," Mr. Poe admonished, a word which here means "reprimanded Klaus even though he was interrupting for a very good reason." "It is not polite to interrupt."

"My name is Stephano," Stephano said, shaking Mr. Poe's hand. "I am—I mean I *was*—Dr. Montgomery's assistant."

"What do you mean *was*?" Mr. Poe asked sternly. "Were you fired?"

"No. Dr. Montgomery—oh, excuse me—" Stephano turned away and pretended to dab at his eyes as if he were too sad to continue. Facing away from Mr. Poe, he gave the orphans a big wink before continuing. "I'm sorry to tell you there's been a horrible accident, Mr. Doe. Dr. Montgomery is dead."

*"Poe,"* Mr. Poe said. "He's dead? That's terrible. What has happened?"

"I don't know," Stephano said. "It looks like snakebite to me, but I don't know anything about snakes. That's why I was going into town, to get a doctor. The children seemed too upset to be left alone."

"He's not taking us to get a doctor!" Klaus shouted. "He's taking us to Peru!"

"You see what I mean?" Stephano said to Mr. Poe, patting Klaus's head. "The children are obviously very distressed. Dr. Montgomery was going to take them to Peru today."

"Yes, I know," Mr. Poe said. "That's why I hurried over here this morning, to finally bring them their luggage. Klaus, I know you're confused and upset over this accident, but please try to understand that if Dr. Montgomery is really dead, the expedition is canceled."

"But Mr. Poe—" Klaus said indignantly.

"Please," Mr. Poe said. "This is a matter for adults to discuss, Klaus. Clearly, a doctor needs to be called."

"Well, why don't you drive on up to the house," Stephano said, "and I'll take the children and find a doctor."

"*José!*" Sunny shrieked, which probably meant something like "No way!"

"Why don't we all go to the house," Mr. Poe said, "and *call* for a doctor?"

Stephano blinked, and for a second his face grew angry again before he was able to calm himself and answer smoothly. "Of course," he said. "I should have called earlier. Obviously I'm not thinking as clearly as you. Here, children, get back in the jeep, and Mr. Poe will follow us."

"We're not getting back in that car with you," Klaus said firmly.

"*Please*, Klaus," Mr. Poe said. "Try to understand. There's been a serious accident. All other discussions will have to be put aside. The only trouble is, I'm not sure my car will start. It's very smashed up."

"Try the ignition," Stephano said. Mr. Poe nodded, and walked back to his car. He sat in the driver's seat and turned the key. The engine made a rough, wet noise—it sounded quite a bit like Mr. Poe's coughs—but it did not start.

"I'm afraid the engine is quite dead," Mr. Poe called out.

"And before long," Stephano muttered to the children, "you will be too."

"I'm sorry," Mr. Poe said. "I couldn't hear you."

Stephano smiled. "I said, that's too bad. Well, why don't I take the orphans back to the house, and you walk behind us? There isn't room for everyone."

Mr. Poe frowned. "But the children's suitcases are here. I don't want to leave them unattended. Why don't we put the luggage into your car, and the children and I will walk back to the house?"

Stephano frowned. "Well, one of the children should ride with me, so I won't get lost."

Mr. Poe smiled. "But you can see the house from here. You won't get lost."

"Stephano doesn't want us to be alone with you," Violet said, finally speaking up. She had been waiting for the proper moment to make her case. "He's afraid that we'll tell you who he really is, and what he's really up to."

"What's she talking about?" Mr. Poe asked Stephano.

"I have no idea, Mr. Toe," Stephano replied, shaking his head and looking at Violet fiercely.

Violet took a deep breath. "This man is not Stephano," she said, pointing at him. "He's Count Olaf, and he's here to take us away."

"Who am I?" Stephano asked. "What am I doing?"

Mr. Poe looked Stephano up and down, and then shook his head. "Forgive the children," he said. "They are very upset. Count Olaf is a terrible man who tried to steal their money, and the youngsters are very frightened of him."

"Do I look like this Count Olaf?" Stephano asked, his eyes shining.

"No, you don't," Mr. Poe said. "Count Olaf had one long eyebrow, and a clean-shaven face. You have a beard, and if you don't mind my saying so, no eyebrows at all."

"He shaved his eyebrow," Violet said, "and grew a beard. Anyone can see that."

"And he has the tattoo!" Klaus cried. "The eye tattoo, on his ankle! Look at the tattoo!"

Mr. Poe looked at Stephano, and shrugged apologetically. "I'm sorry to ask you this," he said, "but the children seem so upset, and before we discuss anything further I'd like to set their minds at ease. Would you mind showing me your ankle?"

"I'd be happy to," Stephano said, giving the children a toothy smile. "Right or left?"

Klaus closed his eyes and thought for a second. "Left," he said.

Stephano placed his left foot on the bumper of Uncle Monty's jeep. Looking at the Baudelaire orphans with his shiny, shiny eyes, he began to raise the leg of his stained striped pants. Violet, Klaus, Sunny, and Mr. Poe all kept their eyes on Stephano's ankle.

The pant leg went up, like a curtain rising to begin a play. But there was no tattoo of an eye to be seen. The Baudelaire orphans stared at a patch of smooth skin, as blank and pale as poor Uncle Monty's face.

## CHAPTER Eight

*While* the jeep sputtered ahead of them, the Baudelaire orphans trudged back toward Uncle Monty's house, the scent of horseradish in their nostrils and a feeling of frustration in their hearts. It is very unnerving to be proven wrong, particularly when you are really right and the person who is really wrong is the one who is proving you wrong and proving himself, wrongly, right. Right?

"I don't know how he got rid of his tattoo," Klaus said stubbornly to Mr. Poe, who was coughing into his handkerchief, "but that's definitely Count Olaf."

"Klaus," Mr. Poe said, when he had stopped coughing, "this is getting very tiresome, going over this again and again. We have just seen Stephano's unblemished ankle. 'Unblemished' means—"

"We *know* what 'unblemished' means," Klaus said, watching Stephano get out of Uncle Monty's jeep and walk quickly into the house. "'Without tattoos.' But it *is* Count Olaf. Why can't you see it?"

"All I can see," Mr. Poe said, "is what's in front of me. I see a man with no eyebrows, a beard, and no tattoo, and that's not Count Olaf. Anyway, even if by some chance this Stephano wishes you harm, you have nothing to fear. It is quite shocking that Dr. Montgomery has died, but we're not simply going to hand over you and your fortune to his assistant. Why, this man can't even remember my name!"

Klaus looked at his siblings and sighed. It

would be easier, they realized, to argue with the snake-shaped hedge than with Mr. Poe when he had made up his mind. Violet was about to try reasoning with him one more time when a horn honked behind them. The Baudelaires and Mr. Poe got out of the way of the approaching automobile, a small gray car with a very skinny driver. The car stopped in front of the house and the skinny person got out, a tall man in a white coat.

"May we help you?" Mr. Poe called, as he and the children approached.

"I am Dr. Lucafont," the tall man said, pointing to himself with a big, solid hand. "I received a call that there's been a terrible accident involving a snake."

"You're here already?" Mr. Poe asked. "But Stephano has scarcely had time to call, let alone for you to drive here."

"I believe that speed is of the essence in an emergency, don't you?" Dr. Lucafont said. "If an autopsy is to be performed, it should be done immediately."

"Of course, of course," Mr. Poe said quickly. "I was just surprised."

"Where is the body?" Dr. Lucafont asked, walking toward the door.

"Stephano can tell you," Mr. Poe said, opening the door of the house. Stephano was waiting in the entryway, holding a coffeepot.

"I'm going to make some coffee," he said. "Who wants some?"

"I'll have a cup," Dr. Lucafont said. "Nothing like a hearty cup of coffee before starting the day's work."

Mr. Poe frowned. "Shouldn't you take a look at Dr. Montgomery first?"

"Yes, Dr. Lucafont," Stephano said. "Time is of the essence in an emergency, don't you think?"

"Yes, yes, I suppose you're right," Dr. Lucafont said.

"Poor Dr. Montgomery is in the Reptile

Room," Stephano said, gesturing to where the Baudelaires' guardian still lay. "Please do a thorough examination, and *then* you may have some coffee."

"You're the boss," Dr. Lucafont said, opening the door of the Reptile Room with an oddly stiff hand. Stephano led Mr. Poe into the kitchen, and the Baudelaires glumly followed. When one feels useless and unable to help, one can use the expression "feeling like a fifth wheel," because if something has four wheels, such as a wagon or a car, there is no real need for a fifth. As Stephano brewed coffee for the adults, the three children sat down at the kitchen table where they had first had coconut cake with Uncle Monty just a short time ago, and Violet, Klaus, and Sunny felt like fifth, sixth, and seventh wheels on a car that was going the wrong direction—toward Hazy Harbor, and the departing *Prospero*.

"When I spoke to Dr. Lucafont on the phone," Stephano said, "I told him about the accident

with your car. When he is done with his medi-
cal examination, he will drive you into town to
get a mechanic and I will stay here with the
orphans."

"No," Klaus said firmly. "We are not staying
alone with him for an instant."

Mr. Poe smiled as Stephano poured him a cup
of coffee, and looked sternly at Klaus. "Klaus, I
realize you are very upset, but it is inexcusable
for you to keep treating Stephano so rudely.
Please apologize to him at once."

"*No!*" Klaus cried.

"That's quite all right, Mr. Yoe," Stephano
said soothingly. "The children are upset over
Dr. Montgomery's murder, so I don't expect
them to be on their best behavior."

"Murder?" Violet said. She turned to Stephano
and tried to look as if she were merely politely
curious, instead of enraged. "Why did you say
*murder*, Stephano?"

Stephano's face darkened, and his hands

clenched at his sides. It looked like there was nothing he wanted to do more than scratch out Violet's eyes. "I misspoke," he said finally.

"Of course he did," Mr. Poe said, sipping from his cup. "But the children can come with Dr. Lucafont and me if they feel more comfortable that way."

"I'm not sure they will fit," Stephano said, his eyes shining. "It's a very small car. But if the orphans would rather, they could come with me in the jeep and we could follow you and Dr. Lucafont to the mechanic."

The three orphans looked at one another and thought hard. Their situation seemed like a game, although this game had desperately high stakes. The object of the game was not to end up alone with Stephano, for when they did, he would whisk them away on the *Prospero*. What would happen then, when they were alone in Peru with such a greedy and despicable person, they did not want to think about. What they had to think about was stopping it from happening. It seemed incredible that their very lives hinged on a carpooling conversation, but in life it is often the tiny details that end up being the most important.

"Why don't we ride with Dr. Lucafont," Violet said carefully, "and Mr. Poe can ride with Stephano?"

"Whatever for?" Mr. Poe asked.

"I've always wanted to see the inside of a doctor's automobile," Violet said, knowing that this was a fairly lame invention.

"Oh yes, me too," Klaus said. "Please, can't we ride with Dr. Lucafont?"

"I'm afraid not," Dr. Lucafont said from the doorway, surprising everyone. "Not all three of you children, anyway. I have placed Dr. Montgomery's body in my car, which only leaves room for two more passengers."

"Have you completed your examination already?" Mr. Poe asked.

"The preliminary one, yes," Dr. Lucafont said.

"I will have to take the body for some further tests, but my autopsy shows that the doctor died of snakebite. Is there any coffee left for me?"

"Of course," Stephano answered, and poured him a cup.

"How can you be sure?" Violet asked the doctor.

"What do you mean?" Dr. Lucafont said quizzically. "I can be sure there's coffee left because I see it right here."

"What I think Violet means," Mr. Poe said, "is how can you be sure that Dr. Montgomery died of snakebite?"

"In his veins, I found the venom of the Mamba du Mal, one of the world's most poisonous snakes."

"Does this mean that there's a poisonous snake loose in this house?" Mr. Poe asked.

"No, no," Dr. Lucafont said. "The Mamba du Mal is safe in its cage. It must have gotten out, bitten Dr. Montgomery, and locked itself up again."

"*What?*" Violet asked. "That's a ridiculous theory. A snake cannot operate a lock by itself."

"Perhaps other snakes helped it," Dr. Lucafont said calmly, sipping his coffee. "Is there anything here to eat? I had to rush over here without my breakfast."

"Your story does seem a little odd," Mr. Poe said. He looked questioningly at Dr. Lucafont, who was opening a cupboard and peering inside.

"Terrible accidents, I have found, are often odd," he replied.

"It can't have been an accident," Violet said. "Uncle Monty is—" She stopped. "Uncle Monty *was* one of the world's most respected herpetologists. He never would have kept a poisonous snake in a cage it could open itself."

"If it wasn't an accident," Dr. Lucafont said, "then someone would have had to do this on purpose. Obviously, you three children didn't kill him, and the only other person in the house was Stephano."

"And I," Stephano added quickly, "hardly know anything about snakes. I've only been working here for two days and scarcely had time to learn anything."

"It certainly appears to be an accident," Mr. Poe said. "I'm sorry, children. Dr. Montgomery seemed like an appropriate guardian for you."

"He was more than that," Violet said quietly. "He was much, much more than an appropriate guardian."

*"That's Uncle Monty's food!"* Klaus cried out suddenly, his face contorted in anger. He pointed at Dr. Lucafont, who had taken a can out of the cupboard. *"Stop eating his food!"*

"I was only going to have a few peaches," Dr. Lucafont said. With one of his oddly solid hands, he held up a can of peaches Uncle Monty had bought only yesterday.

"Please," Mr. Poe said gently to Dr. Lucafont. "The children are very upset. I'm sure you can understand that. Violet, Klaus, Sunny, why don't you excuse yourselves for a little while? We have much to discuss, and you are obviously too overwrought to participate. Now, Dr. Lucafont, let's try and figure this out. You have room for three passengers, including Dr. Montgomery's body. And you, Stephano, have room for three passengers as well."

"So it's very simple," Stephano said. "You and the corpse will go in Dr. Lucafont's car, and I will drive behind you with the children."

"*No,*" Klaus said firmly.

"Baudelaires," Mr. Poe said, just as firmly, "will you three please excuse yourselves?"

"Afoop!" Sunny shrieked, which probably meant "No."

"Of course we will," Violet said, giving Klaus and Sunny a significant look, and taking her siblings' hands, she half-led them, half-dragged them out of the kitchen. Klaus and Sunny looked up at their older sister, and saw that something about her had changed. Her face looked more determined than grief-stricken, and she walked quickly, as if she were late for something.

You will remember, of course, that even years later, Klaus would lie awake in bed, filled with regret that he didn't call out to the driver of the taxicab who had brought Stephano into their lives once more. But in this respect Violet was luckier than her brother. For unlike Klaus, who was so surprised when he first recognized Stephano that the moment to act passed him by, Violet realized, as she heard the adults drone on and on, that the time to act was now. I cannot say that Violet, years later, slept easily when she looked back on her life—there were too many miserable times for any of the Baudelaires to be peaceful sleepers—but she was always a bit proud of herself that she realized she and her siblings should in fact excuse themselves from the kitchen and move to a more helpful location.

"What are we doing?" Klaus asked. "Where are we going?" Sunny, too, looked questioningly at her sister, but Violet merely shook her head in answer, and walked faster, toward the door of the Reptile Room.

## CHAPTER Nine

*When* Violet opened the enormous door
of the Reptile Room, the reptiles
were still there in their cages, the
books were still on their shelves,
and the morning sun was still
streaming through the glass walls, but the
place simply wasn't the same. Even though
Dr. Lucafont had removed Uncle Monty's
body, the Reptile Room was not as invit-
ing as it used to be, and probably never
would be. What happens in a certain
place can stain your feelings for that
location, just as ink can stain a white
sheet. You can wash it, and wash it, and

still never forget what has transpired, a word which here means "happened and made everybody sad."

"I don't want to go in," Klaus said. "Uncle Monty died in here."

"I know we don't want to be here," Violet said, "but we have work to do."

"Work?" Klaus asked. "What work?"

Violet gritted her teeth. "We have work to do," she said, "that Mr. Poe should be doing, but as usual, he is well intentioned but of no real help." Klaus and Sunny sighed as she spoke out loud a sentiment all three siblings had never said, but always felt, since Mr. Poe had taken over their affairs. "Mr. Poe doesn't believe that Stephano and Count Olaf are the same person. And he believes that Uncle Monty's death was an accident. We have to prove him wrong on both counts."

"But Stephano doesn't have the tattoo," Klaus pointed out. "And Dr. Lucafont found the venom of the Mamba du Mal in Monty's veins."

"I know, I know," Violet said impatiently. "The three of us know the truth, but in order to convince the adults, we have to find evidence and proof of Stephano's plan."

"If only we'd found evidence and proof earlier," Klaus said glumly. "Then maybe we could have saved Uncle Monty's life."

"We'll never know about that," Violet said quietly. She looked around at the Reptile Room, which Monty had worked on his whole life. "But if we put Stephano behind bars for his murder, we'll at least be able to prevent him from harming anyone else."

"Including us," Klaus pointed out.

"Including us," Violet agreed. "Now, Klaus, find all of Uncle Monty's books that might contain information about the Mamba du Mal. Let me know when you find anything."

"But all that research could take days," Klaus said, looking at Monty's considerable library.

"Well, we don't have days," Violet said firmly. "We don't even have hours. At five o'clock, the *Prospero* leaves Hazy Harbor, and Stephano is going to do everything he can to make sure we're on that ship. And if we end up alone in Peru with him—"

"All right, all right," Klaus said. "Let's get started. Here, you take this book."

"I'm not taking any book," Violet said. "While you're in the library, I'm going up to Stephano's room to see if I can find any clues."

"Alone?" Klaus asked. "In his room?"

"It'll be perfectly safe," Violet said, although she knew nothing of the kind. "Get cracking with the books, Klaus. Sunny, watch the door and bite anybody who tries to get in."

"Ackroid!" Sunny said, which probably meant something like "Roger!"

Violet left, and true to her word, Sunny sat near the door with her teeth bared. Klaus walked to the far end of the room where the library was, carefully avoiding the aisle where the poisonous snakes were kept. He didn't even want to look at the Mamba du Mal or any other deadly reptile. Even though Klaus knew that Uncle Monty's death was the fault of Stephano and not really of the snake, he could not bear to look at the reptile who had put an end to the happy times he and his sisters had enjoyed. Klaus sighed, and opened a book, and as at so many other times when the middle Baudelaire child did not want to think about his circumstances, he began to read.

It is now necessary for me to use the rather hackneyed phrase "meanwhile, back at the ranch." The word "hackneyed" here means "used by so, so many writers that by the time Lemony Snicket uses it, it is a tiresome cliché." "Meanwhile, back at the ranch" is a phrase used to link what is going on in one part of the story to what is going on in another part of the story, and it has nothing to do with cows or with horses or with any people who work in rural areas where ranches are, or even with ranch dressing, which is creamy and put on salads. Here, the phrase "meanwhile, back at the ranch" refers to what Violet was doing while Klaus and Sunny were in the Reptile Room. For as Klaus began his research in Uncle Monty's library, and Sunny guarded the door with her sharp teeth, Violet was up to something I am sure will be of interest to you.

Meanwhile, back at the ranch, Violet went to listen at the kitchen door, trying to catch what the adults were saying. As I'm sure you know, the key to good eavesdropping is not getting caught, and Violet moved as quietly as she could, trying not to step on any creaky parts of the floor. When she reached the door of the kitchen, she took her hair ribbon out of her pocket and dropped it on the floor, so if anyone opened the door she could claim that she was kneeling down to pick it up, rather than to eavesdrop. This was a trick she had learned when she was very small, when she would listen at her parents' bedroom door to hear what they might be planning for her birthday, and like all good tricks, it still worked.

"But Mr. Poe, if Stephano rides with me in my car, and you drive Dr. Montgomery's jeep," Dr. Lucafont was saying, "then how will you know the way?"

"I see your point," Mr. Poe said. "But I don't think Sunny will be willing to sit on Dr. Montgomery's lap, if he's dead. We'll have to work out another way."

"I've got it," Stephano said. "I will drive the children in Dr. Lucafont's car, and Dr. Lucafont can go with you and Dr. Montgomery in Dr. Montgomery's jeep."

"I'm afraid that won't work," Dr. Lucafont said gravely. "The city laws won't allow anybody else to drive my car."

"And we haven't even discussed the issue of the children's luggage," Mr. Poe said.

Violet stood up, having heard enough to know she had enough time to go up to Stephano's room. Quietly, quietly, Violet walked up the staircase and down the hallway toward Stephano's door, where he had sat holding the knife that fearsome night. When she reached his door, Violet stopped. It was amazing, she thought, how everything having to do with Count Olaf was frightening. He was such a terrible person that merely the sight of his bedroom door could get her heart pounding. Violet found herself half hoping that Stephano would bound up the stairs and stop her, just so she wouldn't have to open this door and go into the room where he slept. But then Violet thought of her own safety, and the safety of her two siblings. If one's safety is threatened, one often finds courage one didn't know one had, and the eldest Baudelaire found she could be brave enough to open the door. Her shoulder still aching from the car collision, Violet turned the brass handle of the door and walked inside.

The room, as Violet suspected, was a dirty mess. The bed was unmade and had cracker crumbs and bits of hair all over it. Discarded newspapers and mail-order catalogs lay on the floor in untidy piles. On top of the dresser was a small assortment of half-empty wine bottles. The closet door was open, revealing a bunch of rusty wire coathangers that shivered in the drafty room. The curtains over the windows were all bunched up and encrusted with something flaky, and as Violet drew closer she realized with faint horror that Stephano had blown his nose on them.

But although it was disgusting, hardened phlegm was not the sort of evidence Violet was hoping for. The eldest Baudelaire orphan stood in the center of the room and surveyed the sticky disorder of the bedroom. Everything was horrendous, nothing was helpful. Violet rubbed her sore shoulder and remembered when she and her siblings were living with Count Olaf and found themselves locked in his tower room. Although it was frightening to be trapped in his inner sanctum—a phrase which here means "filthy room in which evil plans are devised"—it turned out to be quite useful, because they were able to read up on nuptial law and work their way out of their predicament. But here, in Stephano's inner sanctum at Uncle Monty's house, all Violet could find were signs of uncleanliness. Somewhere Stephano must have left a trail of evidence that Violet could find and use to convince Mr. Poe, but where was it? Disheartened—and afraid she had spent too much time in Stephano's bedroom—Violet went quietly back downstairs.

"No, no, no," Mr. Poe was saying, when she stopped to listen at the kitchen door again. "Dr. Montgomery can't drive. He's dead. There must be a way to do this."

"I've told you over and over," Stephano said, and Violet could tell that he was growing angry. "The easiest way is for me to take the three children into town, while you follow with Dr. Lucafont and the corpse. What could be simpler?"

"Perhaps you're right," Mr. Poe said with a sigh, and Violet hurried into the Reptile Room.

"Klaus, Klaus," she cried. "Tell me you've found something! I went to Stephano's room but there's nothing there to help us, and I think Stephano's going to get us alone in his car."

Klaus smiled for an answer and began to read out loud from the book he was holding. "'The Mamba du Mal,'" he read, "'is one of the deadliest snakes in the hemisphere, noted for its strangulatory grip, used in conjunction with its deadly venom, giving all of its victims a tenebrous hue, which is ghastly to behold.'"

"Strangulatory? Conjunction? Tenebrous? Hue?" Violet repeated. "I have no idea what you're talking about."

"I didn't either," Klaus admitted, "until I looked up some of the words. 'Strangulatory' means 'having to do with strangling.' 'In conjunction' means 'together.' 'Tenebrous' means 'dark.' And 'hue' means 'color.' So the Mamba du Mal is noted for strangling people while it bites them, leaving their corpses dark with bruises."

"Stop! Stop!" Violet cried, covering her ears. "I don't want to hear any more about what happened to Uncle Monty!"

"You don't understand," Klaus said gently. "That *isn't* what happened to Uncle Monty."

"But Dr. Lucafont said there was the venom of the Mamba du Mal in Monty's veins," she said.

"I'm sure there was," Klaus said, "but the snake didn't put it there. If it had, Uncle Monty's body would have been dark with bruises. But you and I remember that it was as pale as can be."

Violet started to speak, and then stopped, remembering the pale, pale face of Uncle Monty when they discovered him. "That's true," she said. "But then how was he poisoned?"

"Remember how Uncle Monty said he kept the venoms of all his poisonous snakes in test tubes, to study them?" Klaus said. "I think Stephano took the venom and injected it into Uncle Monty."

"Really?" Violet shuddered. "That's awful."

"Okipi!" Sunny shrieked, apparently in agreement.

"When we tell Mr. Poe about this," Klaus said confidently, "Stephano will be arrested for Uncle Monty's murder and sent to jail. No longer will he try to whisk us away to Peru, or threaten us with knives, or make us carry his suitcase, or anything like that."

Violet looked at her brother, her eyes wide with excitement. "Suitcase!" she said. "His suitcase!"

"What are you talking about?" Klaus said quizzically, and Violet was about to explain when there was a knock on the door.

"Come in," Violet called, signaling to Sunny not to bite Mr. Poe as he walked in.

"I hope you are feeling a bit calmer," Mr. Poe said, looking at each of the children in turn, "and no longer entertaining the thought that Stephano is Count Olaf." When Mr. Poe used the word "entertaining" here he meant "thinking," rather than "singing or dancing or putting on skits."

"Even if he's not Count Olaf," Klaus said carefully, "we think he may be responsible for Uncle Monty's death."

"Nonsense!" Mr. Poe exclaimed, as Violet shook her head at her brother. "Uncle Monty's death was a terrible accident, and nothing more."

Klaus held up the book he was reading. "But while you were in the kitchen, we were reading about snakes, and—"

"Reading about snakes?" Mr. Poe said. "I should think you'd want to read about anything *but* snakes, after what happened to Dr. Montgomery."

"But I found out something," Klaus said, "that—"

"It doesn't matter what you found out about snakes," Mr. Poe said, taking out a handkerchief. The Baudelaires waited while he coughed into it before returning it to his pocket. "It doesn't matter," he said again, "what you found out about snakes. Stephano doesn't know anything about snakes. He told us that himself."

"But—" Klaus said, but he stopped when he saw Violet. She shook her head at him again, just slightly. It was a signal, telling him not to say anything more to Mr. Poe. He looked at his sister, and then at Mr. Poe, and shut his mouth.

Mr. Poe coughed slightly into his handkerchief and looked at his wristwatch. "Now that we have settled that matter, there is the issue of riding in the car. I know that the three of you were eager to see the inside of a doctor's automobile, but we've discussed it over and over and there's simply no way it can work. You three are going to ride with Stephano into town, while I will ride with Dr. Lucafont and your Uncle Monty. Stephano and Dr. Lucafont are unloading all the bags now and we will leave in a few minutes. If you will excuse me, I have to call the Herpetological Society and tell them the bad news." Mr. Poe coughed once more into his handkerchief and left the room.

"Why didn't you want me to tell Mr. Poe what I read?" Klaus asked Violet, when he was sure Mr. Poe was out of earshot, a word which here means "close enough to hear him." Violet didn't answer. She was looking through the glass wall of the Reptile Room, watching Dr. Lucafont and Stephano walk past the snake-shaped hedges to Uncle Monty's jeep. Stephano opened the jeep door, and Dr. Lucafont began to carry suitcases out of the backseat in his strangely stiff hands. "Violet, why didn't you want me to tell Mr. Poe what I read?"

"When the adults come to fetch us," Violet said, ignoring Klaus's question, "keep them in the Reptile Room until I get back."

"But how will I do that?" Klaus asked.

"Create a distraction," Violet answered impatiently, still looking out the window at the little pile of suitcases Dr. Lucafont was making.

"What distraction?" Klaus asked anxiously. "How?"

"For goodness' sake, Klaus," his older sister replied. "You have read hundreds of books. Surely you must have read something about creating a distraction."

Klaus thought for a second. "In order to win the Trojan War," he said, "the ancient Greeks hid soldiers inside an enormous wooden horse. That was sort of a distraction. But I don't have time to build a wooden horse."

"Then you'll have to think of something else," Violet said, and began to walk toward the door, still gazing out the window. Klaus and Sunny looked first at their sister, and then out the window of the Reptile Room in the direction she was looking. It is remarkable that different people will have different thoughts when they look at the same thing. For when the two younger Baudelaires looked at the pile of suitcases, all they thought was that unless they did something quickly, they would end up alone in Uncle Monty's jeep with Stephano. But from the way Violet was staring as she walked out of the Reptile Room, she was obviously thinking something else. Klaus and Sunny could not imagine what it was, but somehow their sister had reached a different conclusion as she looked at her own brown suitcase, or perhaps the beige one that held Klaus's things, or the tiny gray one that was Sunny's, or maybe the large black one, with the shiny silver padlock, that belonged to Stephano.

*When* you were very small, perhaps someone read to you the insipid story—the word "insipid" here means "not worth reading to someone"—of the Boy Who Cried Wolf. A very dull boy, you may remember, cried "Wolf!" when there was no wolf, and the gullible villagers ran to rescue him only to find the whole thing was a joke. Then he cried "Wolf!" when it wasn't a joke, and the villagers didn't come running, and the boy was eaten and the story, thank goodness, was over.

The story's moral, of course, ought to be "Never live somewhere where wolves are running around loose," but whoever read you the story probably told you that the moral was not to lie. This is an absurd moral, for you and I both know that sometimes not only is it good to lie, it is necessary to lie. For example, it was perfectly appropriate, after Violet left the Reptile Room, for Sunny to crawl over to the cage that held the Incredibly Deadly Viper, unlatch the cage, and begin screaming as loudly as she could even though nothing was really wrong.

There is another story concerning wolves that somebody has probably read to you, which is just as absurd. I am talking about Little Red Riding Hood, an extremely unpleasant little girl who, like the Boy Who Cried Wolf, insisted on intruding on the territory of dangerous animals. You will recall that the wolf, after being treated very rudely by Little Red Riding Hood, ate the little girl's grandmother and put on her clothing as a disguise. It is this aspect of the story that is the most ridiculous, because one would think that even a girl as dim-witted as Little Red Riding Hood could tell in an instant the difference between her grandmother and a wolf dressed in a nightgown and fuzzy slippers. If you know somebody very well, like your grandmother or your baby sister, you will know when they are real and when they are fake. This is why, as Sunny began to scream, Violet and Klaus could tell immediately that her scream was absolutely fake.

"That scream is absolutely fake," Klaus said to himself, from the other end of the Reptile Room.

"That scream is absolutely fake," Violet said to herself, from the stairs as she went up to her room.

"My Lord! Something is terribly wrong!" Mr. Poe said to himself, from the kitchen where he was talking on the phone. "Good-bye," he said into the receiver, hung up, and ran out of the kitchen to see what the matter was.

"What's the matter?" Mr. Poe asked Stephano and Dr. Lucafont, who had finished unloading the suitcases and were entering the house. "I heard some screams coming from the Reptile Room."

"I'm sure it's nothing," Stephano said.

"You know how children are," Dr. Lucafont said.

"We can't have another tragedy on our hands," Mr. Poe said, and rushed to the enormous door of the Reptile Room. "Children! Children!"

"In here!" Klaus cried. "Come quickly!" His voice was rough and low, and anyone who didn't know Klaus would think he was very frightened. If you *did* know Klaus, however, you would know that when he was very frightened his voice became tense and squeaky, as it did when he discovered Uncle Monty's body. His voice became rough and low when he was try-ing not to laugh. It is a very good thing that Klaus managed not to laugh as Mr. Poe, Stephano, and

Dr. Lucafont came into the Reptile Room. It would have spoiled everything.

Sunny was lying down on the marble floor, her tiny arms and legs waving wildly as if she were trying to swim. Her facial expression was what made Klaus want to chuckle. Sunny's mouth was wide open, showing her four sharp teeth, and her eyes were blinking rapidly. She was trying to appear to be very frightened, and if you didn't know Sunny it would have seemed genuine. But Klaus *did* know Sunny, and knew that when she was very frightened, her face grew all puckered and silent, as it did when Stephano had threatened to cut off one of her toes. To anyone but Klaus, Sunny looked as if she were very frightened, particularly because of who she was with. For wrapped around Sunny's small body was a snake, as dark as a coal mine and as thick as a sewer pipe. It was looking at Sunny with shiny green eyes, and its mouth was open as if it were about to bite her.

"The Incredibly Deadly Viper!" Klaus cried. "It's going to bite her!" Klaus screamed, and Sunny opened her mouth and eyes even wider to seem even more scared. Dr. Lucafont's mouth opened too, and Klaus saw him start to say something, but he was unable to find words. Stephano, who of course could not have cared less about Sunny's well-being, at least looked surprised, but it was Mr. Poe who absolutely panicked.

There are two basic types of panicking: standing still and not saying a word, and leaping all over the place babbling anything that comes into your head. Mr. Poe was the leaping-and-babbling kind. Klaus and Sunny had never seen the banker move so quickly or talk in such a high-pitched voice. "Goodness!" he cried. "Golly! Good God! Blessed Allah! Zeus and Hera! Mary and Joseph! Nathaniel Hawthorne! Don't touch her! Grab her! Move closer! Run away! Don't move! Kill the snake! Leave it alone! Give it some food! Don't let it bite her!

Lure the snake away! Here, snakey! Here, snakey snakey!"

The Incredibly Deadly Viper listened patiently to Mr. Poe's speech, never taking its eyes off of Sunny, and when Mr. Poe paused to cough into his handkerchief, it leaned over and bit Sunny on the chin, right where it had bitten her when the two friends had first met. Klaus tried not to grin, but Dr. Lucafont gasped, Stephano stared, and Mr. Poe began leaping and babbling again.

"It's bitten her!" he cried. "It bit her! It bited her! Calm down! Get moving! Call an ambulance! Call the police! Call a scientist! Call my wife! This is terrible! This is awful! This is ghastly! This is phantasmagorical! This is—"

"This is nothing to worry about," Stephano interrupted smoothly.

"What do you mean, nothing to worry about?" Mr. Poe asked incredulously. "Sunny was just bitten by—what's the name of the snake, Klaus?"

"The Incredibly Deadly Viper," Klaus answered promptly.

"The Incredibly Deadly Viper!" Mr. Poe repeated, pointing to the snake as it held on to Sunny's chin with its teeth. Sunny gave another fake shriek of fear. "How can you say it's nothing to worry about?"

"Because the Incredibly Deadly Viper is completely harmless," Stephano said. "Calm yourself, Poe. The snake's name is a misnomer that Dr. Montgomery created for his own amusement."

"Are you sure?" Mr. Poe asked. His voice got a little lower, and he moved a bit more slowly as he began to calm down.

"Of course I'm sure," Stephano said, and Klaus recognized a look on his face he remembered from living at Count Olaf's. It was a look of sheer vanity, a word which here means "Count Olaf thinking he's the most incredible person who ever lived." When the Baudelaire orphans had been under Olaf's care, he had often acted this way, always happy to show off his skills, whether he was onstage with his atrocious theater company or up in his tower room making nasty plans. Stephano smiled, and continued to speak to Mr. Poe, eager to show off. "The snake is perfectly harmless—friendly, even. I read up on the Incredibly Deadly Viper, and many other snakes, in the library section of the Reptile Room as well as Dr. Montgomery's private papers."

Dr. Lucafont cleared his throat. "Uh, boss—" he said.

"Don't interrupt me, Dr. Lucafont," Stephano said. "I studied books on all the major species. I looked carefully at sketches and charts. I took careful notes and looked them over each night before I went to sleep. If I may say so, I consider myself to be quite the expert on snakes."

"Aha!" Sunny cried, disentangling herself from the Incredibly Deadly Viper.

"Sunny! You're unharmed!" Mr. Poe cried.

"Aha!" Sunny cried again, pointing at Stephano. The Incredibly Deadly Viper blinked its green eyes triumphantly.

Mr. Poe looked at Klaus, puzzled. "What does your sister mean by 'Aha'?" he asked.

Klaus sighed. He felt, sometimes, as if he had spent half his life explaining things to Mr. Poe. "By 'Aha,'" he said, "she means 'One minute' Stephano claims he knows nothing about snakes, the next he claims he is an expert! By 'Aha' she means 'Stephano has been lying to us.' By 'Aha' she means 'we've finally exposed his dishonesty to you!' By 'Aha' she means *'Aha!'*"

*Meanwhile,* back at the ranch, Violet was upstairs, surveying her bedroom with a critical eye. She took a deep breath, and then tied her hair in a ribbon, to keep it out of her eyes. As you and I and everyone who is familiar with Violet know, when she ties her hair back like that, it is because she needs to think up an invention. And right now she needed to think of one quickly.

Violet had realized, when her brother had talked about Stephano ordering them to carry his suitcase into the

house, that the evidence she had been looking for was undoubtedly in that very suitcase.
And now, while her siblings were distracting the adults in the Reptile Room, would
be her only opportunity to open the suitcase
and retrieve proof of Stephano's evil plot.
But her aching shoulder was a reminder that
she couldn't simply open the suitcase—it was
locked, with a lock as shiny as Stephano's
scheming eyes. I confess that if I were in Violet's
place, with only a few minutes to open a locked
suitcase, instead of on the deck of my friend
Bela's yacht, writing this down, I probably
would have given up hope. I would have sunk
to the floor of the bedroom and pounded
my fists against the carpet wondering why in
the world life was so unfair and filled with
inconveniences.

Luckily for the Baudelaires, however, Violet
was made of sterner stuff, and she took a good
look around her bedroom for anything that

might help her. There wasn't much in the way of inventing materials. Violet longed for a good room in which to invent things, filled with wires and gears and all of the necessary equipment to invent really top-notch devices. Uncle Monty was in fact in possession of many of these supplies, but, to Violet's frustration as she thought of this, they were located in the Reptile Room. She looked at the pieces of butcher paper tacked to the wall, where she had hoped to sketch out inventions as she lived in Uncle Monty's house. The trouble had begun so quickly that Violet had only a few scribblings on one of the sheets, which she had written by the light of a floorlamp on her first night here. Violet's eyes traveled to the floorlamp as she remembered that evening, and when she reached the electric socket she had an idea.

We all know, of course, that we should never, ever, ever, ever, ever, ever, ever, ever, ever,

ever, ever, ever, ever, ever, ever, ever, ever, ever,
ever, ever, ever, ever, ever, ever, ever, ever, ever,
ever, ever, ever, ever, ever, ever, ever, ever, ever,
ever, ever, ever, ever, ever, ever, ever, ever, ever,
ever, ever, ever, ever, ever, ever, ever, ever, ever,
ever, ever, ever, ever, ever, ever, ever, ever, ever,
ever, ever, ever, ever, ever, ever, ever, ever, ever,
ever, ever, ever, ever, ever, ever, ever, ever, ever,
ever, ever, ever, ever, ever, ever, ever, ever, ever,
ever, ever, ever, ever, ever, ever, ever, ever, ever,
ever, ever, ever, ever, ever, ever, ever, ever, ever,
ever, ever, ever, ever, ever, ever, ever, ever, ever,
ever, ever, ever, ever, ever, ever, ever, ever, ever,
ever, ever, ever, ever, ever, ever, ever, ever, ever,
ever, ever, ever, ever, ever, ever, ever, ever, ever,
ever, ever, ever, ever, ever, ever, ever, ever, ever,
ever, ever, ever, ever, ever, ever, ever, ever, ever,
ever, ever, ever, ever, ever, ever, ever, ever, ever,
ever, ever, ever, ever, ever, ever, ever, ever, ever,
ever, ever, ever, ever, ever, ever, ever, ever, ever,
ever, ever, ever, ever, ever, ever, ever, ever, ever,
ever, ever, ever, ever, ever, ever, ever, ever, ever,

ever, *ever* fiddle around in any way with electric devices. *Never.* There are two reasons for this. One is that you can get electrocuted, which is not only deadly but very unpleasant, and the other is that you are not Violet Baudelaire, one of the few people in the world who know how to handle such things. And even Violet was very careful and nervous as she unplugged the lamp and took a long look at the plug itself. It might work.

Hoping that Klaus and Sunny were continuing to stall the adults successfully, Violet wiggled the two prongs of the plug this way and that until at last they came loose from their plastic casing. She now had two small metal strips. Violet then took one of the thumbtacks out of the butcher paper, letting the paper curl down the wall as if it were lazy. With the sharp end of the tack she poked and prodded the two pieces of metal until one was hooked around the other, and then forced the thumbtack between the two pieces so the sharp end stuck straight out. The result looked like a piece of metal you might not notice if it lay in the street, but in fact what Violet had made was a crude—the word "crude" here means "roughly made at the last minute" rather than "rude or ill-mannered"— lockpick. Lockpicks, as you probably know, are devices that work as if they were proper keys, usually used by bad guys to rob houses or escape from jail, but this was one of the rare times when a lockpick was being used by a good guy: Violet Baudelaire.

Violet walked quietly back down the stairs, holding her lockpick in one hand and crossing her fingers with the other. She tiptoed past the enormous door of the Reptile Room and hoped that her absence would not be noticed as she slipped outside. Deliberately averting her eyes from Dr. Lucafont's car to avoid catching even a glimpse of Uncle Monty's body, the eldest Baudelaire walked toward the pile of suitcases. She looked first at the old ones belonging to the Baudelaires. Those suitcases contained, she remembered, lots of ugly, itchy clothing that Mrs. Poe had bought for them soon after their parents died. For a few seconds, Violet found herself staring at the suitcases, remembering how effortless her life had been before all this trouble had set upon them, and how surprising it was to find herself in such miserable circumstances now. This may not be surprising to us, because we know how disastrous the lives of the Baudelaire orphans are, but Violet's misfortune was constantly surprising to her and it took her a minute to push thoughts of their situation out of her head and to concentrate on what she had to do.

She knelt down to get closer to Stephano's suitcase, held the shiny silver padlock in one hand, took a deep breath, and stuck the lockpick into the keyhole. It went inside, but when she tried to turn it around, it scarcely budged, only scraped a little at the inside of the keyhole. It needed to move more smoothly or it would never work. Violet took her lockpick out and wet it with her mouth, grimacing at the stale taste of the metal. Then she stuck the lockpick into the keyhole again and tried to move it. It wiggled slightly and then lay still.

Violet took the lockpick out and thought very, very hard, retying her hair in the ribbon. As she cleared the hair from her eyes, though, she felt a sudden prickle on her skin. It was unpleasant and familiar. It was the feeling of being watched. She looked quickly behind her, but saw only the snake-shaped hedges on the lawn. She looked to the side and saw only the driveway leading down to Lousy Lane. But then she looked straight ahead, through the glass walls of the Reptile Room.

It had never occurred to her that people could see in through the Reptile Room's walls as clearly as they could see out, but when she looked up Violet could see, through the cages of reptiles, the figure of Mr. Poe leaping up and down excitedly. You and I know, of course, that Mr. Poe was panicking over Sunny and the Incredibly

Deadly Viper, but all Violet knew was that what-ever ruse her siblings had devised was still working. The prickle on her skin was not ex-plained, however, until she looked a little closer, just to the right of Mr. Poe, and saw that Stephano was looking right back at her.

Her mouth fell open in surprise and panic. She knew that any second now, Stephano would invent an excuse to leave the Reptile Room and come find her, and she hadn't even opened the suitcase. Quickly, quickly, quickly, she had to find some way to make her lockpick work. She looked down at the damp gravel of the drive-way, and up at the dim, yellowish afternoon sun. She looked at her own hands, smudged with dust from picking apart the electric plug, and that's when she thought of something.

Jumping to her feet, Violet sprinted back into the house as if Stephano were already after her and pushed her way through the door into the kitchen. Shoving a chair to the floor in her haste, she grabbed a bar of soap from the dripping

sink. She rubbed the slippery substance carefully over her lockpick until the entire invention
had a thin, slick coating. Her heart pounding in
her chest, she ran back outside, taking a hurried
look through the walls of the Reptile Room.
Stephano was saying something to Mr. Poe—he
was bragging about his expertise of snakes, but
Violet had no way of knowing that—and Violet
took this moment to kneel down and stick the
lockpick back into the keyhole of the padlock.
It spun quickly all the way around and then
snapped in two, right in her hands. There was
a faint sputter of sound as one half fell to the
grass, the other one sticking in the keyhole like
a jagged tooth. Her lockpick was destroyed.

Violet closed her eyes for a moment in
despair, and then pulled herself to her feet,
using the suitcase to gain her balance. When she
put her hand on the suitcase, however, the padlock swung open, and the case tipped open and
spilled everything all over the ground. Violet fell

back down in surprise. Somehow, as the lock-pick turned, it must have unstuck the lock. Sometimes even in the most unfortunate of lives there will occur a moment or two of good fortune.

It is very difficult, experts have told us, to find a needle in a haystack, which is why "needle in a haystack" has become a rather hackneyed phrase meaning "something that is difficult to find." The reason it is difficult to find a needle in a haystack, of course, is that out of all the things in a haystack, the needle is only one of them. If, however, you were looking for *anything* in a haystack, that wouldn't be difficult at all, because once you started sifting through the haystack you would most certainly find something: hay, of course, but also dirt, bugs, a few farming tools, and maybe even a man who had escaped from prison and was hiding there. When Violet searched through the contents of Stephano's suitcase, it was more like looking for *anything* in a haystack, because she didn't know exactly what she wanted to find. Therefore it was actually fairly easy to find useful items of evidence: a glass vial with a sealed rubber cap, as one might find in a scientific laboratory; a syringe with a sharp needle, like the one your doctor uses to give you shots; a small bunch of folded papers; a card laminated in plastic; a powder puff and small hand mirror.

Even though she knew she had only a few more moments, Violet separated these items from the smelly clothes and the bottle of wine that were also in the suitcase, and looked at all her evidence very carefully, concentrating on each item as if they were small parts out of which she was going to make a machine. And in a way, they were. Violet Baudelaire needed to arrange these pieces of evidence to defeat Stephano's evil plan and bring justice and peace into the lives of the Baudelaire orphans for the first time since their parents perished in the terrible fire. Violet gazed at each piece of evidence, thinking very hard, and before too long, her face lit up the way it always did when all the pieces of something were fit together properly and the machine worked just the way it should.

## CHAPTER Twelve

*I promise* you that this is the last time that I
will use the phrase "meanwhile, back at the
ranch," but I can think of no other way to return
to the moment when Klaus has just explained
to Mr. Poe what Sunny had meant by shouting
"Aha!" and now everyone in the Reptile Room
was staring at Stephano. Sunny looked tri-
umphant. Klaus looked defiant. Mr. Poe looked
furious. Dr. Lucafont looked worried. You

couldn't tell how the Incredibly Deadly Viper looked, because the facial expressions of snakes are difficult to read. Stephano looked back at all these people silently, his face fluttering as he tried to decide whether to come clean, a phrase which here means "admit that he's really Count Olaf and up to no good," or perpetuate his deception, a phrase which here means "lie, lie, lie."

"Stephano," Mr. Poe said, and coughed into his handkerchief. Klaus and Sunny waited impatiently for him to continue. "Stephano, explain yourself. You have just told us that you are an expert on snakes. Previously, however, you told us you knew nothing of snakes, and therefore couldn't have been involved in Dr. Montgomery's death. What is going on?"

"When I told you I knew nothing of snakes," Stephano said, "I was being modest. Now, if you will excuse me, I have to go outside for a moment, and—"

"You weren't being modest!" Klaus cried.

"You were *lying!* And you are lying now! You're nothing but a liar and murderer!"

Stephano's eyes grew wide and his face clouded in anger. "You have no evidence of that," he said.

"Yes we do," said a voice in the doorway, and everyone turned around to find Violet standing there, with a smile on her face and evidence in her arms. Triumphantly, she walked across the Reptile Room to the far end, where the books Klaus had been reading about the Mamba du Mal were still stacked in a pile. The others followed her, walking down the aisles of reptiles. Silently, she arranged the objects in a line on top of a table: the glass vial with the sealed rubber cap, the syringe with the sharp needle, the small bunch of folded papers, a card laminated in plastic, the powder puff and the small hand mirror.

"What is all this?" Mr. Poe said, gesturing to the arrangement.

"This," Violet said, "is evidence, which I

found in Stephano's suitcase."

"My suitcase," Stephano said, "is private property, which you are not allowed to touch. It's very rude of you, and besides, it was locked."

"It was an emergency," Violet said calmly, "so I picked the lock."

"How did you do that?" Mr. Poe asked. "Nice girls shouldn't know how to do such things."

"My sister *is* a nice girl," Klaus said, "and she knows how to do all sorts of things."

"Roofik!" Sunny agreed.

"Well, we'll discuss that later," Mr. Poe said. "In the meantime, please continue."

"When Uncle Monty died," Violet began, "my siblings and I were very sad, but we were also very suspicious."

"We weren't suspicious!" Klaus exclaimed. "If someone is suspicious, it means they're not sure! We were *positive* that Stephano killed him!"

"Nonsense!" Dr. Lucafont said. "As I explained to all of you, Montgomery Montgomery's death was an accident. The Mamba du Mal escaped from its cage and bit him, and that's all there is to it."

"I beg your pardon," Violet said, "but that is *not* all there is to it. Klaus read up on the Mamba du Mal, and found out how it kills its victims."

Klaus walked over to the stack of books and opened the one on top. He had marked his place with a small piece of paper, so he found what he was looking for right away. "'The Mamba du Mal,'" he read out loud, "'is one of the deadliest snakes in the hemisphere, noted for its strangulatory grip, used in conjunction with its deadly venom, giving all of its victims a tenebrous hue, which is ghastly to behold.'" He put the book down, and turned to Mr. Poe. "'Strangulatory' means—"

"We *know* what the words mean!" Stephano shouted.

"Then you must know," Klaus said, "that the Mamba du Mal did not kill Uncle Monty. His body didn't have a tenebrous hue. It was as pale as could be."

"That's true," Mr. Poe said, "but it doesn't necessarily indicate that Dr. Montgomery was murdered."

"Yes," Dr. Lucafont said. "Perhaps, just this once, the snake didn't feel like bruising its victim."

"It is more likely," Violet said, "that Uncle Monty was killed with these items." She held up the glass vial with the sealed rubber cap. "This vial is labeled 'Venom du Mal,' and it's obviously from Uncle Monty's cabinet of venom samples." She then held up the syringe with the sharp needle. "Stephano—Olaf—took this syringe and injected the venom into Uncle Monty. Then he poked an extra hole, so it would look like the snake had bitten him."

"But I loved Dr. Montgomery," Stephano said. "I would have had nothing to gain from his death."

Sometimes, when someone tells a ridiculous

lie, it is best to ignore it entirely. "When I turn eighteen, as we all know," Violet continued, ignoring Stephano entirely, "I inherit the Baudelaire fortune, and Stephano intended to get that fortune for himself. It would be easier to do so if we were in a location that was more difficult to trace, such as Peru." Violet held up the small bunch of folded papers. "These are tickets for the *Prospero*, leaving Hazy Harbor for Peru at five o'clock today. That's where Stephano was taking us when we happened to run into you, Mr. Poe."

"But Uncle Monty tore up Stephano's ticket to Peru," Klaus said, looking confused. "I saw him."

"That's true," Violet said. "That's why he had to get Uncle Monty out of the way. He killed Uncle Monty—" Violet stopped for a minute and shuddered. "He killed Uncle Monty, and took this laminated card. It's Monty's membership card for the Herpetological Society. Stephano planned to pose as Uncle Monty to

get on board the *Prospero*, and whisk us away to
Peru."

"But I don't understand," Mr. Poe said. "How
did Stephano even know about your fortune?"

"Because he's really Count Olaf," Violet said,
exasperated that she had to explain what she
and her siblings and you and I knew the
moment Stephano arrived at the house. "He
may have shaved his head, and trimmed off his
eyebrows, but the only way he could get rid of
the tattoo on his left ankle was with this powder puff and hand mirror. There's makeup all
over his left ankle, to hide the eye, and I'll bet
if we rub it with a cloth we can see the tattoo."

"That's absurd!" Stephano cried.

"We'll see about that," Mr. Poe replied.
"Now, who has a cloth?"

"Not me," Klaus said.

"Not me," Violet said.

"Guweel!" Sunny said.

"Well, if nobody has a cloth, we might as well
forget the whole thing," Dr. Lucafont said, but

Mr. Poe held up a finger to tell him to wait. To the relief of the Baudelaire orphans, he reached into his pocket and withdrew his handkerchief.

"Your left ankle, please," he said sternly to Stephano.

"But you've been coughing into that all day!" Stephano said. "It has germs!"

"If you are really who the children say you are," Mr. Poe said, "then germs are the least of your problems. Your left ankle, please."

Stephano—and this is the last time, thank goodness, we'll have to call him by his phony name—gave a little growl, and pulled his left pants leg up to reveal his ankle. Mr. Poe knelt down and rubbed at it for a few moments. At first, nothing appeared to happen, but then, like a sun shining through clouds at the end of a terrible rainstorm, the faint outline of an eye began to appear. Clearer and clearer it grew until it was as dark as it had been when the orphans first saw it, back when they had lived with Count Olaf.

Violet, Klaus, and Sunny all stared at the eye, and the eye stared back. For the first time in their lives, the Baudelaire orphans were happy to see it.

*CHAPTER*
## Thirteen

*If* this were a book written to entertain small children, you would know what would happen next. With the villain's identity and evil plans exposed, the police would arrive on the scene and place him in a jail for the rest of his life, and the plucky youngsters would go out for pizza and live happily ever after. But this book is about the Baudelaire orphans, and you and I know that these three unfortunate children living happily ever after is about as likely as Uncle Monty returning to life. But it seemed to the Baudelaire orphans, as the tattoo became evident, that at least a little bit of Uncle Monty had come back to them as they proved Count Olaf's treachery once and for all.

"That's the eye, all right," Mr. Poe said, and stopped rubbing Count Olaf's ankle. "You are most definitely Count Olaf, and you are most definitely under arrest."

"And I am most definitely shocked," Dr. Lucafont said, clapping his oddly solid hands to his head.

"As am I," Mr. Poe agreed, grabbing Count Olaf's arm in case he tried to run anywhere. "Violet, Klaus, Sunny—please forgive me for not believing you earlier. It just seemed too far-fetched that he would have searched you out, disguised himself as a laboratory assistant, and concocted an elaborate plan to steal your fortune."

"I wonder what happened to Gustav, Uncle Monty's *real* lab assistant?" Klaus wondered out loud. "If Gustav hadn't quit, then Uncle Monty never would have hired Count Olaf."

Count Olaf had been quiet this whole time, ever since the tattoo had appeared. His shiny eyes had darted this way and that, watching everyone carefully the way a lion will watch a herd of antelope, looking for the one that would be best to kill and eat. But at the mention of Gustav's name, he spoke up.

"Gustav didn't quit," he said in his wheezy voice. "Gustav is *dead!* One day when he was out collecting wildflowers I drowned him in the Swarthy Swamp. Then I forged a note saying he quit." Count Olaf looked at the three children as if he were going to run over and strangle them, but instead he stood absolutely still, which somehow was even scarier. "But that's nothing compared to what I will do to you, orphans. You have won this round of the game, but I will return for your fortune, and for your precious skin."

"This is not a game, you horrible man," Mr.

Poe said. "Dominos is a game. Water polo is a game. Murder is a crime, and you will go to jail for it. I will drive you to the police station in town right this very minute. Oh, drat, I can't. My car is wrecked. Well, I'll take you down in Dr. Montgomery's jeep, and you children can follow along in Dr. Lucafont's car. I guess you'll be able to see the inside of a doctor's automobile, after all."

"It might be easier," Dr. Lucafont said, "to put Stephano in my car, and have the children follow behind. After all, Dr. Montgomery's body is in my car, so there's no room for all three children, anyway."

"Well," Mr. Poe said, "I'd hate to disappoint the children after they've had such a trying time. We can move Dr. Montgomery's body to the jeep, and—"

"We couldn't care less about the inside of a doctor's automobile," Violet said impatiently. "We only made that up so we wouldn't be trapped alone with Count Olaf."

"You shouldn't tell lies, orphans," Count Olaf said.

"I don't think you are in a position to give moral lectures to children, Olaf," Mr. Poe said sternly. "All right, Dr. Lucafont, *you* take him."

Dr. Lucafont grabbed Count Olaf's shoulder with one of his oddly stiff hands, and led the way out of the Reptile Room and to the front door, stopping at the doorway to give Mr. Poe and the three children a thin smile.

"Say good-bye to the orphans, Count Olaf," Dr. Lucafont said.

"Good-bye," Count Olaf said.

"Good-bye," Violet said.

"Good-bye," Klaus said.

Mr. Poe coughed into his handkerchief and gave a sort of disgusted half-wave at Count Olaf, indicating good-bye. But Sunny didn't say anything. Violet and Klaus looked down at her, surprised that she hadn't said "Yeet!" or "Libo!" or any of her various terms for "good-bye." But Sunny was staring at Dr. Lucafont with a determined look in her eye, and in a moment she had leaped into the air and bitten him on the hand.

"Sunny!" Violet said, and was about to apologize for her behavior when she saw Dr. Lucafont's whole hand come loose from his arm and fall to the floor. As Sunny clamped down on it with her four sharp teeth, the hand made a crackling sound, like breaking wood or plastic rather than skin or bone. And when Violet looked at the place where Dr. Lucafont's hand had been, she saw no blood or indication of a wound, but a shiny, metal hook. Dr. Lucafont looked at the hook, too, and then at Violet, and grinned horribly. Count Olaf grinned too, and in a second the two of them had darted out the door.

"The hook-handed man!" Violet shouted. "He's not a doctor! He's one of Count Olaf's henchmen!" Instinctively, Violet grabbed the air where the two men had been standing, but of course they weren't there. She opened the front door wide and saw the two of them sprinting through the snake-shaped hedges.

"After them!" Klaus shouted, and the three Baudelaires started to run through the door. But Mr. Poe stepped in front of them and blocked their way.

"No!" he cried.

"But it's the hook-handed man!" Violet shouted. "He and Olaf will get away!"

"I can't let you run out after two dangerous criminals," Mr. Poe replied. "I am responsible for the safety of you children, and I will not have any harm come to you."

"Then *you* go after them!" Klaus cried. "But hurry!"

Mr. Poe began to step out the door, but he stopped when he heard the roar of a car engine starting up. The two ruffians—a word which here means "horrible people"—had reached Dr. Lucafont's car, and were already driving away.

"Get in the jeep!" Violet exclaimed. "Follow them!"

"A grown man," Mr. Poe said sternly, "does not get involved in a car chase. This is a job for the police. I'll go call them now, and maybe they can set up roadblocks."

The Baudelaire youngsters watched Mr. Poe shut the door and race to the telephone, and their hearts sank. They knew it was no use. By the time Mr. Poe was through explaining the situation to the police, Count Olaf and the hook-handed man were sure to be long gone. Suddenly exhausted, Violet, Klaus, and Sunny walked to Uncle Monty's enormous staircase and sat down on the bottom step, listening to the faint sound of Mr. Poe talking on the phone. They knew that trying to find Count Olaf and the hook-handed man, particularly when it grew dark, would be like trying to find a needle in a haystack.

Despite their anxiety over Count Olaf's escape, the three orphans must have fallen asleep for a few hours, for the next thing they knew, it was nighttime and they were still on the bottom step. Somebody had placed a blanket over them, and as they stretched themelves, they saw three men in overalls walking out of the Reptile Room, carrying some of the reptiles in their cages. Behind them walked a chubby man in a brightly colored plaid suit, who stopped when he saw they were awake.

"Hey, kids," the chubby man said in a loud, booming voice. "I'm sorry if I woke you up, but my team has to move quickly."

"Who are you?" Violet asked. It is confusing to fall asleep in the daytime and wake up at night.

"What are you doing with Uncle Monty's rep-tiles?" Klaus asked. It is also confusing to realize you have been sleeping on stairs, rather than in a bed or sleeping bag.

"Dixnik?" Sunny asked. It is always confusing why anyone would choose to wear a plaid suit.

"The name's Bruce," Bruce said. "I'm the

director of marketing for the Herpetological Society. Your friend Mr. Poe called me to come and retrieve the snakes now that Dr. Montgomery has passed on. 'Retrieve' means 'take away.'"

"We *know* what the word 'retrieve' means," Klaus said, "but why are you taking them? Where are they going?"

"Well, you three are the orphans, right? You'll be moving on to some other relative who won't die on you like Montgomery did. And these snakes need to be taken care of, so we're giving them away to other scientists, zoos, and retirement homes. Those we can't find homes for we'll have put to sleep."

"But they're Uncle Monty's collection!" Klaus cried. "It took him years to find all these reptiles! You can't just scatter them to the winds!"

"It's the way it has to be," Bruce said smoothly. He was still talking in a very loud voice, for no apparent reason.

"Viper!" Sunny shouted, and began to crawl toward the Reptile Room.

"What my sister means," Violet explained, "is that she's very close friends with one of the snakes. Could we take just one with us—the Incredibly Deadly Viper?"

"First off, *no*," Bruce said. "That guy Poe said all the snakes now belong to us. And second off, if you think I'm going to let small children near the Incredibly Deadly Viper, think again."

"But the Incredibly Deadly Viper is harmless," Violet said. "Its name is a misnomer."

Bruce scratched his head. "A what?"

"That means 'a wrong name,'" Klaus explained. "Uncle Monty discovered it, so he got to name it."

"But this guy was supposed to be brilliant," Bruce said. He reached into a pocket in his plaid jacket and pulled out a cigar. "Giving a snake a wrong name doesn't sound brilliant to me. It sounds idiotic. But then, what can you expect from a man whose own name was Montgomery Montgomery?"

"It is not nice," Klaus said, "to lampoon someone's name like that."

"I don't have time to ask you what 'lampoon' means," Bruce said. "But if the baby here wants to wave bye-bye to the Incredibly Deadly Viper, she'd better do it soon. It's already outside."

Sunny began to crawl toward the front door, but Klaus was not through talking to Bruce. "Our Uncle Monty *was* brilliant," he said firmly.

"He was a brilliant man," Violet agreed, "and we will always remember him as such."

"Brilliant!" Sunny shrieked, in mid-crawl, and her siblings smiled down at her, surprised she had uttered a word that everyone could understand.

Bruce lit his cigar and blew smoke into the air, then shrugged. "It's nice you feel that way, kid," he said. "Good luck wherever they put you." He looked at a shiny diamond watch on his wrist, and turned to talk to the men in overalls. "Let's get a move on. In five minutes we have to be back on that road that smells like ginger."

"It's *horseradish*," Violet corrected, but Bruce had already walked away. She and Klaus looked at each other, and then began following Sunny outside to wave good-bye to their reptile friends. But as they reached the door, Mr. Poe walked into the room and blocked them again.

"I see you're awake," he said. "Please go upstairs and go to sleep, then. We have to get up very early in the morning."

"We just want to say good-bye to the snakes," Klaus said, but Mr. Poe shook his head.

"You'll get in Bruce's way," he replied. "Plus, I would think you three would never want to see a snake again."

The Baudelaire orphans looked at one another and sighed. Everything in the world seemed wrong. It was wrong that Uncle Monty was dead. It was wrong that Count Olaf and the hook-handed man had escaped. It was wrong for Bruce to think of Monty as a person with a silly name, instead of a brilliant scientist. And it was wrong to assume that the children never wanted to see a snake again. The snakes, and indeed everything in the Reptile Room, were the last reminders the Baudelaires had of the few happy days they'd spent there at the house—the few happy days they'd had since their parents had perished. Even though they understood that Mr. Poe wouldn't let them live alone with the reptiles, it was all wrong never to see them again, without even saying good-bye.

Ignoring Mr. Poe's instructions, Violet, Klaus, and Sunny rushed out the front door where the men in overalls were loading the cages into a van with "Herpetological Society" written on the back. It was a full moon, and the moonlight reflected off the glass walls of the Reptile Room as though it were a large jewel with a bright, bright shine—*brilliant*, one might say. When Bruce had used the word "brilliant" about

Uncle Monty, he meant "having a reputation for cleverness or intelligence." But when the children used the word—and when they thought of it now, staring at the Reptile Room glowing in the moonlight—it meant more than that. It meant that even in the bleak circumstances of their current situation, even throughout the series of unfortunate events that would happen to them for the rest of their lives, Uncle Monty and his kindness would shine in their memories. Uncle Monty was brilliant, and their time with him was brilliant. Bruce and his men from the Herpetological Society could dismantle Uncle Monty's collection, but nobody could ever dismantle the way the Baudelaires would think of him.

"Good-bye, good-bye!" the Baudelaire orphans called, as the Incredibly Deadly Viper was loaded into the truck. "Good-bye, good-bye!" they called, and even though the Viper was Sunny's special friend, Violet and Klaus found themselves crying along with their sister, and when the Incredibly Deadly Viper looked up to see them, they saw that it was crying too, tiny shiny tears falling from its green eyes. The Viper was brilliant, too, and as the children looked at one another, they saw their own tears and the way they shone.

"You're brilliant," Violet murmured to Klaus, "reading up on the Mamba du Mal."

"You're brilliant," Klaus murmured back, "getting the evidence out of Stephano's suitcase."

"Brilliant!" Sunny said again, and Violet and Klaus gave their baby sister a hug. Even the youngest Baudelaire was brilliant, for distracting the adults with the Incredibly Deadly Viper.

"Good-bye, good-bye!" the brilliant Baudelaires called, and waved to Uncle Monty's reptiles. They stood together in the moonlight, and kept waving, even when Bruce shut the doors of the van, even as the van drove past the snake-shaped hedges and down the driveway to Lousy Lane, and even when it turned a corner and disappeared into the dark.

**LEMONY SNICKET** was born in a small town where the inhabitants were suspicious and prone to riot. He now lives in the city. During his spare time he gathers evidence and is considered something of an expert by leading authorities.

**BRETT HELQUIST** was born in Ganado, Arizona, grew up in Orem, Utah, and now lives in New York City. He earned a bachelor's degree in fine arts from Brigham Young University and has been illustrating ever since. His art has appeared in many publications, including *Cricket* magazine and *The New York Times*.

To My Kind Editor,

I am writing to you from the shores of
Lake Lachrymose, where I am examining the
remains of Aunt Josephine's house in order
to completely understand everything that
happened when the Baudelaire orphans found
themselves here.

Please go to the Café Kafka at 4 P.M.
next Wednesday and order a pot of jasmine
tea from the tallest waiter on duty.
Unless my enemies have succeeded, he will
bring you a large envelope instead.
Inside the envelope, you will find my
description of these horrific events,
entitled THE WIDE WINDOW, as well as a
sketch of Curdled Cave, a small bag of
shattered glass, and the menu from the
Anxious Clown restaurant. There will also
be a test tube containing one (1)
Lachrymose Leech, so that Mr. Helquist
can draw an accurate illustration. UNDER
NO CIRCUMSTANCES should this test tube be
opened.

Remember, you are my last hope that
the tales of the Baudelaire orphans can
finally be told to the general public.

With all due respect,

*Lemony Snicket*

Lemony Snicket